THE
RINGMASTER'S
DAUGHTER

Also by Jostein Gaarder

THE RINGMASTER'S DAUGHTER

Jostein Gaarder

Translated by James Anderson

Weidenfeld & Nicolson
London

A PHOENIX HOUSE BOOK

First published in English in Great Britain in 2002 by
Phoenix House

Copyright © H. Aschehoug & Co (W. Nygaard) AS, Oslo 2001
Translated from the original Norwegian edition *Sirkusdirektoerens datter*

English translation © James Anderson 2002

A CIP catalogue record for this book is
available from the British Library.

All author's royalties from this book will be donated to the Sophie Foundation.
The Sophie Foundation awards the annual Sophie Prize (100,000 US dollars)
for outstanding achievement in working towards a sustainable future.

www.sophieprize.org

ISBN 0 297 82923 8

Typeset at The Spartan Press Ltd,
Lymington, Hants

Printed in Great Britain by
Clays Ltd, St Ives plc

Phoenix House
Weidenfeld & Nicolson
The Orion Publishing Group Ltd
Orion House
5 Upper St Martin's Lane
London WC2H 9EA

My brain is seething. I'm bubbling with hundreds of new ideas. They just keep welling up.

Perhaps it's possible to control thoughts to a certain extent, but to stop thinking is asking too much. My head is teeming with beguiling notions, I'm not able to fix them before they're ousted by new thoughts. I can't keep them apart.

I'm rarely able to remember my thoughts. Before I manage to dwell on one of my inspirations, it generally melts into an even better idea, but this, too, is so fickle of character that I struggle to save it from the constant volcanic stream of new ideas . . .

Once more my head is full of voices. I feel haunted by an excitable swarm of souls who use my brain cells to talk to one another. I haven't the equanimity to harbour them all, some must be racked off. I have a considerable intellectual surplus and I constantly need to unburden it. At regular intervals I have to sit down with pencil and paper and relieve myself of ideas . . .

When I awoke a few hours ago, I was certain I'd formulated the world's most competent adage. Now I'm not so sure, but at least I've given the virginal aphorism a due place in my notebook. I am convinced it could be traded for a better dinner. If I sold it to someone who already has a name, it might make it into the next edition of Familiar Quotations.

At last I've decided what I want to be. I shall continue doing what I've always done, but from now on I'll make a living out of it. I

don't feel the need to be famous, that's an important consideration,
but I could still become extremely rich.

I feel sad as I leaf through this old diary. I was nineteen when
the entries above, dated 10 and 12 December 1971, were
written. Maria had left for Stockholm several days before,
she was three or four weeks pregnant. In the years that
followed we met a few times, but now it's been twenty-six
years since I last saw her. I don't know where she lives, I
don't even know if she's still alive.

If she could see me now. I had to jump aboard an early
morning flight and get away from it all. In the end, the
external pressure built up to something like the one inside
me, and so an equilibrium was achieved. I can think more
clearly now. If I'm careful I may be able to live here for a
few weeks before the net tightens around me for good.

I'm thankful I got away from the Book Fair in one piece.
They followed me to the airport, but I doubt if they were
able to discover which plane I boarded. I bought the first
empty seat out of Bologna. 'Don't you know where you
want to go?' I shook my head. 'I just want to go away,' I
said. 'On the first plane.' Now it was her turn to shake her
head, then she laughed. 'We don't get many like you,' she
said, 'but there'll be a lot more in the future, believe me.'
And then, when I'd paid for my ticket: 'Have a good
holiday! I'm sure you deserve it . . .'

If only she'd known. If only she'd known what I
deserved.

Twenty minutes after my plane had taken off, another
one left for Frankfurt. I wasn't on it. I'm sure they imagined
I was heading home for Oslo, with my tail between my legs.
But it isn't always wise to take the shortest route home if
your tail is between your legs.

★

I've put up at an old inn on the coast. I sit staring out across the sea. On a promontory down by the shore stands an old Moorish tower. I watch the fishermen in their blue boats. Some are still in the bay, hauling in their nets, others are moving towards the breakwater with the day's catch.

The floor is tiled. The chill strikes up through my feet. I've put three pairs of socks on, but they're useless against these cold floor tiles. If things don't improve soon, I'll pull the counterpane off the big double bed and fold it to use as a foot-rest.

I ended up here quite by chance. The first plane out of Bologna could just as easily have been for London or Paris. But I feel it's even more of a coincidence that, as I write, I'm leaning over an old writing table where once, long ago, another Norwegian – who was also an exile of sorts – sat and wrote. I'm staying in a town which was one of the first places in Europe to start manufacturing paper. The ruins of the old paper-mills are still strung out like pearls on a string along the valley bottom. They must be inspected, of course. But as a rule I ought to keep to the hotel. I've taken full board.

It's unlikely anyone in these parts has heard of The Spider. Here everything revolves around tourism and lemon growing, and fortunately both are out of season. I see that some visitors are paddling in the sea, but the bathing season hasn't yet begun and the lemons need a few more weeks to ripen.

There is a phone in my room, but I have no friends to confide in, there have been none since Maria left. I could hardly be labelled a friendly person, or a decent one, but I do at least have one acquaintance who doesn't wish me dead. There was an article in the *Corriere della Sera*, he said, and after that everything seemed to start falling apart. I decided

3

to get away early next morning. On the flight south I had leisure enough to think back. I am the only one who knows the full and complete extent of my activities.

I've decided to tell all. I write in order to understand myself and I shall write as honestly as I can. This doesn't mean that I'm reliable. The man who passes himself off as reliable in anything he writes about his own life has generally capsized before he's even set out on that hazardous voyage.

As I sit thinking, a small man paces about the room. He's only a metre tall, but he's fully grown. The little man is dressed in a charcoal-grey suit and black patent leather shoes, he wears a high-crowned, green felt hat and, as he walks, he swings a small bamboo cane. Now and then he points his cane up at me, and this signifies that I must hurry up and begin my story.

It is the little man with the felt hat who has urged me to confess everything I can remember.

It will certainly be more difficult to kill me once my memoirs are out. The mere rumour that they are being penned would sap the courage of even the boldest. I'll ensure that such a rumour is circulated.

Several dozen dictaphone cassettes have been securely deposited in a bank box – there, now that's out – I won't say where, but my affairs are in order. I've collected almost one hundred voices on these tiny cassettes, so these already have an acknowledged motive for murdering me. Some have made open threats, it's all on the cassettes, which are numbered consecutively from I to XXXVIII. I have also devised an ingenious index that makes it easy to locate any one of the voices. I have been prudent, some might even call it cunning. I'm certain that hearsay about the cassettes has saved my skin for a couple of years now. Supplemented by these jottings, the little miracles will have even greater value.

I don't mean to imply that my confessions, or the cassettes, will be any guarantee of safe conduct. I imagine I'll travel on to South America, or somewhere in the East. Just now I find thoughts of a Pacific island alluring. I'm insular anyway, I've always been insular. To me there's something more pathetic about being isolated in a big city than on a small island in the Pacific.

I became wealthy. It was no surprise to me. I may well be the very first person in history to have plied my particular trade, at least in such a big way. The market has been limitless, and I've always had merchandise to sell. My business wasn't illegal, I even paid a certain amount of tax. I lived modestly, too, and can now afford to pay substantial tax arrears should the matter ever arise. It wasn't an unlawful trade from my customers' point of view either, just dishonourable.

I realise that from this day forth I'll be poorer than most because I'll be on the run. But I wouldn't have swapped my life for that of a teacher. I wouldn't have swapped it for an author's life, either. I'd have found it hard to live with a definite career.

The little man is making me nervous. The only way to forget him is to get on with my writing. I'll begin as far back as I can remember.

Little Petter Spider

I believe I had a happy childhood. My mother didn't think so. She was informed of Petter's unsociable behaviour even before he started school.

The first serious chat my mother was summoned to, was at the day nursery. I'd sat there all morning just watching the other children play. But I hadn't felt bad. It had amused me to see how intensely they lived. Many children find it fun to watch lively kittens, canaries or hamsters; I did too, but it was even more fun to watch lively children. And then, I was the one controlling them, I was the one deciding everything they did or said. They didn't realise it themselves, neither did the nursery assistant. Sometimes I'd have a temperature and have to stay at home and listen to the Stock Exchange prices. At times like these nothing at all would happen at the day nursery. The children would just keep getting in and out of their jump suits, in and out. I didn't envy them. I don't think they even had any elevenses.

I only saw my father on Sundays. We went to the circus. The circus wasn't bad, but when I got home I'd begin to plan a circus of my own. That was far better. It was before I'd learnt to write, but I assembled my own favourite circus in my head. No problem there. I drew the circus as well, not just the big top and the seats, but all the animals and circus performers too. That was hard. I wasn't good at drawing. I gave up drawing long before I began school.

I sat on the big rug barely moving a muscle, and my mother asked me several times what I was thinking about. I said I was playing circuses, which was the truth. She asked if we oughtn't to play something else.

'The girl on the trapeze is called Panina Manina,' I said. 'She's the ringmaster's daughter. But no one at the circus knows it, not even her, or the ringmaster.'

My mother listened intently, she turned the radio down, and I went on: 'One day she falls off the trapeze and breaks her neck. It's the final performance, when there aren't any more people in town who want to buy tickets for the circus. The ringmaster stoops over the poor girl, and just then he sees she has a slender chain around her neck. On the chain is an amber trinket, and inside the trinket is a spider that's millions of years old. When he sees this, the ringmaster realises that Panina Manina is his own daughter, because he bought her that rare trinket on the day she was born.'

'So at least he knew he had a daughter,' my mother interjected.

'But he thought she'd drowned,' I explained. 'You see, the ringmaster's daughter fell into the River Aker when she was eighteen months old. At the time she was just plain Anne-Lise. After that the ringmaster had no idea she was still alive.'

My mother's eyes widened. It was as if she didn't believe my story, so I said: 'But luckily she was saved from the freezing cold water by a fortune-teller who lived all alone in a pink caravan by the river, and from that day on the ringmaster's daughter lived in the caravan together with the fortune-teller.'

My mother had lit a cigarette. She stood there disporting herself in a tight-fitting costume. 'Did they really live in a caravan?'

I nodded. 'The ringmaster's daughter had lived in a circus trailer ever since she'd been born. So she'd have found it far stranger to move into a modern block of flats on an estate.

The fortune-teller had no idea what the little girl's name was, so she christened her Panina Manina, the name she's kept to this day.'

'But how did she get back to the circus?' my mother asked.

'She grew up,' I said. 'That's easy enough to understand. Then she went to the circus on her own two feet. That wasn't the least bit difficult, either. This all happened before she became paralysed!'

'But she could hardly remember that her father was a ringmaster,' my mother protested.

I felt a pang of despair. It wasn't the first time my mother had disappointed me; she really could be quite dense.

'We've been over this already,' I said. 'I told you that she didn't know she was the ringmaster's daughter, and the ringmaster didn't know either. Of course he couldn't recognise his daughter when he hadn't seen her since she was one and a half.'

My mother thought I should rethink that part, but there was no need. 'On the day the fortune-teller fished the ringmaster's daughter from the river, she stared into her crystal ball and foretold that the little girl would become a famous circus performer and so, one fine day, the girl made her way to the circus on her own two feet. Everything a real fortune-teller sees in her crystal ball will always come true. That was why the fortune-teller gave the girl a circus name, and taught her some fine trapeze tricks, too, to be on the safe side.'

My mother had stubbed her cigarette out in an ashtray on the green piano. 'But why did the fortune-teller need to teach her . . . ?'

I cut in: 'When Panina Manina arrived at the circus and demonstrated her abilities, she was given a job on the spot, and soon she was as famous as Abbott and Costello. But the ringmaster still had no idea she was his daughter. If he had, he certainly wouldn't have allowed her to do all those risky stunts on the trapeze.'

'Well, I give up,' my mother said. 'Shall we go for a walk in the park?'

But I went on: 'The fortune-teller's crystal ball had also told her that Panina Manina would break her neck at the circus, and a genuine prophecy is impossible to avert. So she packed up all her belongings and went to Sweden.'

My mother had gone into the kitchen to fetch something. Now she was standing in front of the piano with a large cabbage in her hand. It most definitely wasn't a crystal ball.

'Why did she go to Sweden?' she asked in amazement.

I'd thought about that. 'So that the ringmaster and the fortune-teller wouldn't have to bicker about who Panina Manina should live with after she'd broken her neck and couldn't look after herself any more,' I said.

'Did the fortune-teller know that the ringmaster was the girl's father?' my mother asked.

'Not until Panina Manina was on her way to the circus,' I explained. 'Only then did the crystal ball tell her that the girl would be reunited with her father just after she'd broken her neck, and so the old lady might as well take her caravan and move to Sweden. She thought it was wonderful that Panina Manina was going to be reunited with her father, but not quite so wonderful that she had to break her neck before he recognised her.'

I was in a bit of a quandary about how to continue. Not because it was difficult, quite the opposite, but simply because there were so many possibilities to choose from. 'Now Panina Manina sells candy-floss at the circus from a wheelchair,' I said. 'It's a special kind of candy-floss that makes everyone laugh so much at the clowns that they can hardly catch their breath. And once there was a boy who really couldn't. He thought it was fun to laugh at the clowns, but not quite so funny to lose his breath.'

This was really the end of Panina Manina's story. I'd already begun the story of the boy who laughed so much that he lost his breath. And there were lots of other circus performers to consider. I was responsible for the entire circus.

My mother didn't realise this. 'I suppose Panina Manina had a mother too?' she said.

'No,' I said (or, to be accurate, I think I screamed it). 'She was dead as a matter of fact!'

And then I began to cry. Perhaps I cried for a whole hour. As always, it was my mother who comforted me. I didn't cry because the story was sad. I cried because I was scared of my own imagination. I was also afraid of the little man with the bamboo stick. He'd been perched on the Persian pouffe during my narrative, looking at my mother's gramophone records, but now he'd begun to pace about the room. I was the only one who could see him.

The first time I'd set eyes on the little man in the green hat had been in a dream. But he broke out of the dream and since then he's followed me all my life. He thinks *he's* in charge of *me*.

It was all too easy to make things up, it was like skating on thin ice, it was like doing dainty pirouettes on a brittle crust over water thousands of fathoms deep. There was always something dark and cold that lay beckoning beneath the surface.

★

I've never had any difficulty telling imagination and reality apart. The problem has always been to distinguish between recalled fantasy and recalled reality. That's quite another matter. I always knew the difference between what I was actually observing and what I only imagined I was observing. But gradually, as time went by, separating actual occurrences from experiences I'd made up, could get tricky. My memory hasn't got special compartments for things I've seen and heard and things I've simply conjured up. I've only got one memory in which to store both the impressions and imaginings of the past: in glorious unity they combine to form what we call recollection. Despite this, I sometimes assume that my memory is failing when I occasionally mix up the two categories. This is an imperfect description at best. When I recollect something as really experienced, that in truth was only a dream, it's because my memory is far too good. I've always felt it a triumph of memory that I'm capable of recalling events that have only taken place in my own head.

I was often at home alone. My mother was at her job in the City Hall until late in the afternoon, and sometimes she went out visiting female friends. I never hung about with other children, I preferred not to. Activities with friends were nothing compared to all the things I could find to do on my own.

I've always liked my own company best. The few boring episodes I recall from my childhood were always spent in the company of others of my own age. I remember their dull, nit-picking games. I sometimes said I had to hurry home because we were expecting guests. It wasn't true.

I remember well the first time some boys rang the doorbell and asked if I wanted to come out and play. Their clothes were dirty, one of them had a snotty nose, and there they were, asking me if I wanted to come out and play cowboys and Indians. I pretended I had a stomach ache, or gave some other, more plausible excuse. I couldn't see the point of playing cowboys and Indians round the cars and drying racks. I could play the game far better in my own imagination where there were real horses and tomahawks, rifles and bows and arrows, cowboys, chiefs and medicine men. I could sit in the kitchen or in the living room and, without lifting a finger, stage the most colourful battles between braves and palefaces, and I was always on the side of the Indians. These days almost everyone is on the side of the Indians, but it's rather too late now. Even when I was three or four years old I made sure the Yankees got some stiff resistance. Without my efforts there might not be a single Indian reservation around today.

The boys tried again on several occasions. They wanted me to join them in tossing pennies, playing marbles or football or shooting peas, but this urge to get me outside tailed off pretty quickly. Soon, there were no more scampering feet on the stairs. I don't think anyone called for me after I was eight or nine years old. Now and again, I would sit behind the Venetian blind in the kitchen and spy on them. It could be amusing at times, but I never felt the need for any physical contact with my peers.

Only the onset of puberty broke this mould. From the age of twelve I began to think of lots of things I could get up to with a girl of my own age, or one considerably older for that matter. Yearning made me restless, but no girl ever came and rang our doorbell and asked me if I'd like to go out with her. I'd have had little objection to accompanying a girl I liked on a trip to the woods or to the Newt Pond.

I didn't feel lonely until there was something to yearn for. Loneliness and longing are two sides of the same coin.

When I was at home by myself I made regular use of the telephone, almost always to make what I called 'silly calls'. High up on the list of silly calls were taxis. I once rang for six taxis to go to the same address on the other side of the road. It was really comical to sit at the kitchen window watching all the cabs turning up. Soon all the taxi-drivers jumped out and began to talk to one another. They must have thought they were picking up guests from some huge coffee morning. Finally, one of them went to the entrance of the flats and rang the ground floor bell. But there was no Mrs Nielsen living there. That was news to them, but not to me. They stood there gesticulating, and then clambered back into their taxis and drove off at top speed. One of them stayed behind and looked around as if he was standing on a great stage. But he didn't catch sight of any audience. Perhaps he thought only God could see him. I sat there squinting down at him through the slats of the Venetian blind, I smiled, I sipped at a glass of Simpson's orange juice, but the man didn't stir. He might at least have got into his cab and turned the meter off.

Calling up taxis to go to other parts of town was fun as well. It was amusing to think of my taxis setting off and driving round the city even though I couldn't actually watch them myself. I saw them clearly enough in my head, and that was almost as priceless as seeing the real thing. Sometimes I called up ambulances and fire engines as well. Once I phoned the police and said I'd seen a dead man in the nearby paddock. I had to give my name, my address and which school I went to. It was easy, I just made something up. I knew that the police car had to drive past our block to get to the paddock. It passed us after only eight minutes, and two minutes later an ambulance drove past as well. They were my cars.

I'm quite certain all this is recalled reality. The black telephone on the little table in the hall was a constant temptation. Sometimes I'd just plonk myself down on the spindle-backed chair by the hall table and dial a number at random. Until 4 p.m. it was almost invariably women who answered, and when I'd got a woman on the line, I'd disguise my voice and ask, for example, how often she and her husband screwed. I'd ask if she'd screwed with other men too. Or I'd introduce myself as a Customer Consultant for Saba de Luxe. I used to see how long it took the women to hang up. As a rule it was over in a few seconds, but I once talked to a woman for more than half an hour. After that I couldn't be bothered to go on – there were limits – and I asked something so impertinent that even she had to give up. 'I've never heard the like,' she exclaimed. No, you certainly haven't, I thought, as she slammed the phone down. How privileged she'd been to speak to me for more than half an hour!

Sometimes I made up long tales to feed to the women I spoke to. For instance, I might spin a yarn about how Mum and Dad had taken the boat to England and gone off to London, leaving me on my own at home for ten days even though I was only seven. I might add that, now we'd got a fridge, Mum had left me lots of food, but that I couldn't get anything to eat because I was scared of sharp kitchen knives. Or I might kick off the conversation by saying that my father was away grouse shooting and that my mother was desperately ill in bed, too ill to speak. Provided I gave my name and address, the offers of emergency aid and assistance were limitless. But naturally, I couldn't divulge such sensitive information. So it was better to say that a little man had made me ring just for fun. 'He's only a metre tall and he's rushing around the flat,' I might say, 'and if I don't do what he says, he'll beat me with his stick.'

Once my mother complained about the phone bill. She

was truly distracted, so I owned up at once. I explained that I often telephoned the lady who spoke the time even though I knew what it was. I said I used to ring the talking clock again and again just because I was bored. I pretended I didn't know that the voice wasn't that of a real woman. I said I was trying to get her to answer me and that was why I phoned again and again. By the time I'd finished speaking, my mother had forgiven me. I'd been banking on that. We agreed that from then on I'd limit myself to two calls per day, and it was a promise I kept. I didn't even regard it as a curb. Now I had to think carefully about who I wanted to talk to. It was even better. Working out who I wanted to phone was almost as entertaining as phoning itself. There was no waste of call units after that.

I'm fifty per cent sure that I once spoke to the Prime Minister, Einar Gerhardsen. But that could as easily be fantasy recall. I am, however, one hundred per cent certain that I rang the Nora factory and complained about buying a bottle of pop that tasted of vinegar. I know this for a fact, because several days later a whole case of the stuff arrived on our doorstep. I told my mother I'd won it in a competition at the shop. She asked lots of questions, which was good, because I had to make up answers all the time. I think my mother liked this kind of intelligent conversation too. She wouldn't let it drop until she was absolutely convinced I was telling the truth.

On one particular occasion I had an interesting conversation with King Olav. We agreed to take a long skiing trip together as neither of us knew anyone we enjoyed going out with. He told me over the phone that he found being a king boring, and then asked me if I thought it was childish of him to want to buy a gigantic model railway and set it up in the palace ballroom. I said I thought it a marvellous idea provided I was allowed to help him build it. He had to promise it would be a Märklin train set and at least four times the size of the model railway in the Science Museum. I knew that the king was far richer than the Science Museum. I had a steam engine and a Meccano set, but no Märklin model railway.

I'm ninety-nine per cent certain that this business with the king is remembered fantasy. Which doesn't mean it isn't true. The model railway that the king and I built at the palace in the weeks that followed, was just as real as the sun and moon. To this day I retain an exact picture of the final layout, I can still see all the tunnels and viaducts, points and sidings. In the end we had more than fifty different loco-motives, almost all with lights.

One day the Crown Prince came in and insisted we remove the whole lot because he and his young friends wanted to use the ballroom for a party. The Crown Prince was fifteen years my senior and I respected him deeply, but it did seem unreasonable that he should suddenly start giving the king orders. It was a breach of tradition, if nothing else. When the king and I didn't agree to clear away the layout immediately, the Crown Prince quickly returned with a large pot of yoghurt which he proceeded to hurl at it. The pot disintegrated, of course, and the yoghurt splattered all over the layout so that it began to resemble a snowy landscape, though it didn't smell much like a winter walk in the woods. From then on there was no train service at the palace.

★

Because she worked at City Hall, my mother often got free tickets to theatres and cinemas. She was always given two tickets, and since she and my father couldn't stand the sight of each other, I had to go with her. It meant she didn't have to track down a baby-sitter. I'd worn out many a baby-sitter.

We always used to dress up to go to the theatre, and my mother would often hold a little fashion parade for my benefit before making up her mind which costume or dress to wear. My mother called me her little escort. It was I who'd take off her coat and hand it to the cloakroom attendant. It was I who'd keep the matches in my jacket pocket and light her cigarettes, and when she found someone to talk to in the interval, it was I who'd stand in the queue to get the drinks. On one occasion I was about to buy a fizzy orange for myself and a Cinzano for my mother, but the woman behind the bar refused to give me the glass of Cinzano even though my mother was winking energetically at her from only a few feet away. The woman said she wasn't allowed to serve Cinzano to children, so would my mother please come to the bar and collect the drink herself. That made my mother hopping mad. Not many children went to adult plays and my mother knew that the woman behind the bar recognised me.

After we'd been to a theatre or cinema, I always used to tell my mother how the play or film could have been vastly improved. Sometimes I'd say straight out that I thought a play was bad. I never said it was boring, I never thought the theatre was boring. Even a poor play was fun to watch – if nothing else, live people were performing – and if the play was really bad, I was in my element, because then we had masses to talk about on the way home.

My mother didn't like me saying that a play was bad. I think she'd rather I'd said it was boring.

When we got home from a theatre or cinema, we quite often sat in the kitchen and continued the discussion there. My mother would light candles and make something nice to eat. It might be something quite ordinary like bread with saveloy sausage and pickled gherkins, but my favourite was steak tartare sandwich with raw egg yolk and capers. My mother thought I was too young to like capers – it was something we discussed lots of times – but I believe, deep down, she enjoyed the fact that I had a taste for capers at such a tender age. The only thing she didn't like was when I said a play was bad, or that such and such a director was awful.

I always read the programme thoroughly – after all, it was written for me – and naturally I knew the names of the principal performers. My mother thought I was taking things a bit far, though, when I got to know the names of all the designers too. But I was her escort, and so she had to accept it. During the performance I might whisper the name of the stage manager to her, at least if anything went wrong during the show.

On one occasion, in Ibsen's *A Doll's House*, Nora's dress fell down – it just slid off right in front of Dr Rank. They were all alone in the drawing room, and Dr Rank's last line made it extra funny that Nora lost her dress in that particular scene. 'And what other delights am I to see?' asked Dr Rank. 'You'll see nothing more, because you're not nice,' replied Nora. She tore herself away from the doctor and just then her dress fell off. I leant towards mother and whispered the name of the dresser in her ear.

Once when we'd sat far into the night discussing a play, I told my mother that I thought she looked like Jacqueline Kennedy. I believe my mother enjoyed hearing that, and it wasn't just something I'd hit on to flatter her. I really did think my mother was almost the spitting image of Jacqueline Kennedy.

When I was eleven, my mother and I went to see Chaplin's film *Limelight*. Watching that film turned me into an adult. The first time I felt the desire to do things to a girl considerably older than me was when I saw Claire Bloom in the role of the unhappy ballet dancer. The second time was when I watched Audrey Hepburn playing Eliza in *My Fair Lady*. My mother had got tickets for the Norwegian premiere.

I was particularly fond of Chaplin, not least because of his film music, and especially the well-known theme in *Limelight*, even though the first few bars were just an inversion of the exposition of Tchaikovsky's piano concerto in B minor. The melody 'Smile' from *Modern Times* was little better: it was nothing more than a minor key variation of a Russian folk melody. I also suspected Chaplin of stealing some musical ideas from Puccini, who was capable of being just as melodramatic. But it was all to the good that Chaplin had found inspiration in other composers, because I loved both Tchaikovsky and Puccini, and so did my mother. We went to the opera and saw *Madam Butterfly*. I tried not to cry, but it wasn't easy. My throat didn't choke with sobs because Pinkerton leaves Madam Butterfly, or because she kills herself in the end – I knew she was going to do that from the start of act two. It was the music that had me fighting back the tears, right from the moment in the first act when Madam Butterfly comes over the crest of the hill with the great choir of women. I was only twelve at the time, but the picture of all those women with their colourful parasols singing on the path up from Nagasaki, haunts me still.

At home we played *La Bohème* with Jussi Björling and Victoria de los Angeles on the gramophone, and my mother always began sniffling when Musetta drags in the sick Mimi in act four. Then I'd go into another room, leaving the door open behind me. Not because I wanted to hear my mother crying, but because I was listening to the music. And then I could shed some tears of delight, too.

Before I'd seen Chaplin's *Limelight*, Puccini and Tchaikovsky were the only real geniuses I'd encountered. When I was at home by myself, I would play the final movement of the *Symphonie Pathétique*. It would have been very embarrassing if my mother had found me out. I was big enough to like capers, but even I had to admit that I was a bit young to be in raptures over classical music. I tried to play the music at full volume whilst keeping an ear out for my mother on the stairs. Sometimes the little man would stand by the front door and listen for footsteps down in the lobby.

I had read about Tchaikovsky in the encyclopaedia. He had died of cholera just a few days after he'd given the first performance of the *Symphonie Pathétique*. His life's work was complete. After the first performance of the *Symphonie Pathétique* he no longer bothered to sterilise his drinking water. He'd written his own requiem, and now he had no more tunes left inside him. He was finished with this world. I, too, felt rather finished with the world when the last chords of the *Symphonie Pathétique* faded away.

Death was something my mother and I never talked about. I never talked to her about girls either. I was just as careful to conceal a *Playboy* magazine as I'd been to cover up listening to the *Symphonie Pathétique*.

I was only seven when we saw *East of Eden* with James Dean as Cal. My mother almost broke down at the end of the film when Cal's girlfriend has to beg his father to love him. 'It hurts not to be loved,' she said. 'It makes people evil. Show him that you love him. Try! Please!'

Cal's father hated his son because he thought the boy had taken his mother's part when she'd left her husband and children and become a steely brothel-keeper. Before he died he did manage a reconciliation with his son. He told him to send the nurse away. 'I want *you* to look after me,' he said. It was the same as saying that he loved his son.

My mother found it hard to speak about that film. I

realised she was the one who'd told my father to move out. That wasn't normal in those days. It was rare for a mother with a small child to throw the father out of their flat.

As I was going to bed that evening, she suggested we ask my father to Sunday lunch. It was all right by me, but nothing came of it, and I wasn't going to nag her into picking up the phone and inviting him.

I had certain vague, almost dreamlike impressions of things that had happened in the flat before my father left. It is possible to remember the atmosphere of a dream without actually being able to break the dream itself. I knew there was something cold and hard that I was trying to repress, and so well did I consign it to oblivion that I could no longer remember what it was I was trying to forget.

The only thing I recalled about that time was some mysterious things I'd dreamt about a man who was exactly my height, but who was nevertheless a real, grown-up man with a hat and a stick and that, suddenly one morning, he'd appeared in the flat in broad daylight. He'd moved into our flat around the same time my father moved out.

I imagined that perhaps there was someone out in dreamland who was missing him. Possibly the little man had left his wife and children too, or perhaps he'd been kicked out of the fairy tale where he belonged because he'd misbehaved. But it was also feasible that he commuted between two realities. I wondered whether the little man sneaked back to dreamland during the night while I was asleep. That wouldn't be so strange, because I certainly went there when I slept. The really odd thing was that the little fellow was capable of swaggering about the flat in the middle of the day.

I was the only person in my class with divorced parents. But the father of one of the girls was a communist, and Hans Olav's dad had been in prison.

Having divorced parents wasn't a problem. I preferred being with them one at a time. I also think I got better Christmas presents from my mother and father than other children got from their parents. I always got two presents. My mother and father couldn't even co-operate over gifts. On the contrary, I think they vied to give me the nicer present. They never gave anything to each other.

My father took me to watch skating heats and ski-jumping. He was an expert on lap times and form ratings. It's not his fault I've turned out the way I have. We went to Holmenkollen to watch the three ski-jumping Ts: Toralf Engan, Torbjørn Yggeseth and Torgeir Brandtzæg. They jumped before Wirkola, the supreme champion. That was easy. Jumping *before* Wirkola wasn't difficult.

When I was eight, my father and I took the boat to Copenhagen. We only spent one night there, but that evening we went to the Tivoli Gardens. I thought I'd been to an amusement park before, but the Tivoli in Copenhagen was worlds away from 'Ivar's Tivoli' in Oslo. I felt like a tourist from some Third World country. What must Danish children think of us Norwegians when they go to 'Ivar's Tivoli' in Oslo, I wondered in horror and dismay.

My father was in high spirits. I think he was feeling rather proud of himself for getting me out of the country and a safe distance away from my mother. On the ship he'd said in a man-to-man sort of way that a few days to herself would do my mother the world of good. It wasn't true, I felt sure she wanted to come to Copenhagen with me, but it had obviously been out of the question once my father had proposed that he and I should go. I think my father knew that I'd really rather have gone to the Tivoli Gardens with my mother. Then my mother and I could have strolled amongst the crowds and gossiped about the things we saw and thought. My mother and I often had identical notions. Or we could have gone to a café and had a nice chat.

My father's trouser pockets were full of Danish money and he wanted us to ride the dodgems and the ghost train, the merry-go-round and the big dipper, the Ferris wheel and the tunnel of love. I was only eight, but I was acutely aware of the embarrassment of having to do the tunnel of love with my father, bad breath and all. It was awful being jammed in a little boat with him, listening to artificial birdsong in a tunnel full of paper flowers and pastel shades. I think my father felt pretty pained as well, because he didn't utter a word. I was scared he might suddenly put his arm around me and say something like: 'Isn't this lovely, son? Don't you think so, Petter?' The worst thing of all was that I felt convinced it was just what he wanted to do, only he didn't dare put his arm round my shoulders because he knew I wouldn't like it. Perhaps that was why neither of us spoke.

It was mainly for my father's sake that I went on all the rides. I was more interested in going round looking at everything the Tivoli Gardens contained. I'd made up my mind to note every detail, right down to each little tombola and hot-dog stand. From the very first instant I'd known that this visit would entail a lot of work when I got back, I'd been seriously inspired. I walked around thinking that soon I'd be going home to create the world's finest amusement park. This was after I'd given up drawing, so I had to make an effort to remember exactly how everything was. In the end I succeeded in forming a detailed picture of Copenhagen's Tivoli Gardens, but I had to draw it in my head, I had to get it all off pat. It wasn't easy to concentrate, because now and then I had to look up at my father and say something to him too – he mustn't think I was moping. Just before we left, I won a soft toy in the shape of a red tiger. I gave it to a little girl who was crying. My father thought I was being kind, he didn't realise that I wasn't interested in red, cuddly tigers. If my mother had seen me win such a thing, she'd have given one of her characteristic peals of laughter.

Even before our visit to the Gardens had come to an end, I'd mentally constructed a ghost train with everything from dangling skeletons to ghosts and monsters. But I'd also positioned a real live man in the middle of my tunnel, a perfectly ordinary man in a hat and coat, who might, for instance, be eating a carrot. I imagined that the people riding the ghost train would give an extra, ear-piercing scream when they suddenly caught sight of a real person in the tunnel.

In certain situations the sight of a live person can be as scary as that of a ghost, especially in a ghost tunnel. Ghosts inhabit the imagination, and if something real enters the imagination, it can seem almost as eerie as if some fantasy figure had suddenly loomed up in real life.

I was truly frightened the first time I saw that little man with his bamboo stick outside the confines of a dream, but the novelty soon wore off. If elves and trolls began to stream out of the woods all of a sudden, we'd naturally be alarmed, but sooner or later we would get used to them. We'd have to.

Once I dreamt I'd found a purse containing four silver dollars. I'd have been pretty shaken if I'd woken up and found myself holding that same purse in my hand. I'd have had to try to convince myself that I was still asleep, and then make another attempt to wake up.

We think we're awake even when we're dreaming, but

we *know* we're awake when we're not sleeping. I had a theory that the little man with the walking-stick lay sleeping somewhere in dreamland and only dreamt that he inhabited reality. Even at the time of my visit to the Tivoli Gardens I was a good bit taller than him. I'd begun to call him Metre Man because he was only a metre tall.

I said nothing about these new rides to my father; I wasn't trying to complain. Perhaps it was a bit unfair that the result of all this inspiration was to blossom in my mother's vicinity: she became more and more jealous because my father was the one who'd taken me to Copenhagen. 'You've got amusement parks on the brain,' she said a few days after I got home. I observed that perhaps that was because I'd been a huge tivoli in a previous life. My mother laughed. 'You mean you worked in a huge tivoli in a previous life,' she said. I shook my head and emphasised that I'd actually been an entire amusement park.

★

I took plenty of punishment as a child. It was never my father who hit me, or my mother.

I reckoned that the reason I never got smacked by them, was that they were divorced. Because they didn't share the same house they could never agree about when I deserved punishment. My mother was only too painfully aware that if she were hard on me, my father would be the first to hear about it. Sometimes I'd ring my father and ask if I could stay up an hour or two longer than my mother had decreed. He always supported me when he glimpsed an opportunity of making me happy and my mother cross at the same time, thus completing his satisfaction. And when I needed more money than my mother was willing to give me, I would also ring my father. My father was never angry. He only saw me once a week. We agreed this was enough.

It was the boys at school who beat me up, and that wasn't much to boast about, because I wasn't big or strong. They called me Little Petter Spider. When I'd been younger, my father and I had visited the Geological Museum and we'd seen a piece of amber with a spider, millions of years old, embedded in it, and I'd mentioned this spider at school on one occasion. We'd been learning about electricity and I informed the class that the word 'electricity' was derived from the Greek word for 'amber'. From then on I was known only as Little Petter Spider.

Though small in stature, I had a big mouth. That was why I got beaten up. I was especially glib when there were adults close by or when I was just about to hop on a bus or lock myself into the flats. I could get so carried away at moments like these that I never gave a thought to the following day. I wasn't good at what is now called forward-planning, I never took the trouble to make a risk assessment. I would come face to face with the boys again, of course, and when I did there wasn't always a grown-up about.

I was much more skilful with words than my peers, and better at telling stories too. I found it easier to express myself than many of the pupils who were three and four classes above me. This brought me many a bruise. There was too little emphasis on freedom of speech in those days. We'd learnt about human rights at school, but we were never reminded that freedom of speech applies just as much to children and amongst children.

On one occasion, Ragnar sent me hurtling into a drying rack so hard that it cut my head open. As soon as I began to bleed I found the courage to say a whole lot of things I'd otherwise have kept to myself. I dished up some startling home truths about Ragnar's family – for example, that his father was always getting drunk with down-and-outs – and Ragnar didn't retaliate now. He could at least have answered my accusations, but Ragnar wasn't much good at talking, he just stood there and stared at me bleeding. So I called him a cowardy custard who didn't dare shut me up because everything I said was true. I claimed to have once seen him devouring dog turds. Next, I said that his mother had to wash him on a big changing mat in the living-room because he pissed and shitted in his trousers. Everyone knew his mother bought nappies at the shop, I observed. She bought so many she got a discount. Blood was pouring from my head. Four or five boys stood watching me solemnly. My hand told me that my hair was all wet. I felt cold. I said that the whole street knew that Ragnar's father was a country bumpkin. I also knew, I said, why he'd moved to the city. It was a secret that even Ragnar might not be privy to, but one that I would willingly divulge now. Ragnar's father had to move to Oslo because he'd been arrested by the police, and the reason he'd been arrested was that he'd been screwing sheep. He screwed them so much that many of the sheep got ill, I said. They got screwing sickness, acute screwing sickness, and one of the sheep had even died of it. That sort of thing's not too popular, I revealed, not even north of Oslo. After this last piece of information they all ran off. I wasn't quite sure if this was due to the sheep north of Oslo or the blood pouring from my head. But now there was a big pool of it on the tarmac at my feet. It surprised me that the blood near my brain was so viscous and sticky. I'd imagined it to be a shade brighter and a little thinner than other blood. For some moments my gaze shifted to a luminous sign over the basement entrance. *BOMB SHEL-TER* it said in large, green letters, and I tried to read the words backwards, but the green letters just made me feel queasy. Suddenly Metre Man came rushing round the corner of the building. I was already a head and a half taller than him. He looked up at me with a startled expression, pointed up at my hair with his bamboo stick and exclaimed: *'Well, well! What now?'*

I felt unhappy about returning to my mother, because I knew she hated the sight of blood, and especially mine. But I had no choice. As soon as I got in, my mother wrapped my head in cotton towels until I looked like an Arab, and we took a taxi to Accident & Emergency. I had to have twelve stitches. The doctor said that was the record for the day. Afterwards we went home and had pancakes.

This is recalled reality. I still have a broad scar on my forehead. It's not the only scar I incurred. I've got several similar 'distinguishing marks'. Now, at least, they've stopped noting that sort of thing on my passport.

Of course my mother wanted to know what had happened. I said I'd got into a fight with a boy I didn't know because he said that my dad screwed sheep. For once my mother took pity on my father. She was usually the first to slag him off behind his back, but a line had to be drawn somewhere. I think she saw something noble in my defence of my father's honour. 'I can see why you got angry, Petter,' was all she said. 'One doesn't say that sort of thing. I quite agree.'

I never told tales. Telling tales was like mimicking real events. It was far too banal. Squealing or lashing out was only for people who weren't good at expressing themselves.

★

I got thumped less once we began to get homework. That was because I helped the other pupils in the class with their tasks. I never sat down and did school work with them –

that would have been far too boring, and I was frightened of making friends. But it became more and more usual for me to do my own homework first and, when I'd finished that, to do the same thing once or twice more. It was these extra answers that I could give away or sell for a bar of chocolate or an ice-cream to one of the others in the class.

As a rule we could choose between three or four essay subjects. When, for example, I'd written the story 'Almost an Adventure', I'd get an itch to do the essay entitled 'When the Lights Went Out' as well. But I wasn't allowed to hand in both essays. So I could give one of them away to Tore or Ragnar.

Helping Tore and Ragnar with their homework was a good idea, because then they wouldn't beat me up. That wasn't principally out of gratitude. I think they were frightened I'd announce to the class that I'd done their essays for them. Saying so wouldn't get me into trouble with the teacher. It wasn't my fault we were only allowed to give one answer each. And I hadn't handed in Tore's or Ragnar's work. They had appropriated these essays themselves. It was obvious.

I never went round touting such extra pieces of work, but gradually classmates would approach me and ask if they could purchase some assistance. A number of transactions took place this way, and they weren't always done for money or chocolate, but often for quite different sorts of returns. It might be nothing more than a couple of obscene words in a needlework class or a snowball placed on the teacher's chair. I remember such homework help continuing to the age when a task could be bartered with one of the boys in return for the loosening of a female classmate's bra strap. Only one or two girls in our class had begun to use a bra, and they weren't the nicest ones. While such favours remained outstanding the debtor was in danger, as I might eventually feel myself obliged to tell the teacher that I'd taken it upon myself to help Øivind or Hans Olav with his homework.

Homework help wasn't limited to Norwegian. I could offer written answers in geography, religious instruction, local history and maths. All that mattered was that they weren't too similar to my own answers. First, I'd do my own maths homework without any errors. Thereafter it didn't take long to work up a couple more sets of answers, but this time I had to insert the requisite number of errors in the sums. It wouldn't have been at all plausible for Tore to hand in homework that was totally error free. Tore was satisfied with a C+, so I had to prepare a C+ answer. If someone else also wanted a C+ answer, it had to be of the same standard, but obviously the mistakes couldn't be the same.

It wasn't that uncommon for me to produce homework for a D or D+. There was a market at this standard too. I well understood why Arne and Lisbeth couldn't be bothered to do homework when the results never produced more than a D+ or a C−. However, I never took any payment for D answers, there had to be a limit. I considered it payment enough to do them. I was particularly fond of producing answers with lots of mistakes. They required more ingenuity than unblemished ones. They demanded more imagination.

If I was really strapped for cash, and my mother and father were on speaking terms for once and neither would grant me more than my regular pocket money, I would occasionally produce a B–A or even an A. I believe I once even managed to deliver an A+ in geography for Hege, who was a championship dancer at Åse and Finn's Dancing School and was practising like mad for a samba and cha-cha-cha competition. On such occasions I would often introduce a small error into my own offering, and thus aim for a B+ so as not to eclipse the other answer. Then the teacher would write 'A little lacking in concentration, Petter?' – or something in that vein. It was all so amusing. Even then, in the early sixties, a few teachers had introduced what later became known as 'differentiation'. Maintaining that an answer meriting a B+ was lacking in concentration was a differentiated comment. Had it been Lisbeth's work, he would have written 'Congratulations, Lisbeth! A really solid piece of homework.' The teacher didn't know that I'd made the mistake for fun. He didn't realise I'd cheated just to get a worse mark.

The upshot was that Hege had to read her exceptional geography task to the entire class. She hadn't reckoned on that, but the teacher was adamant that she go up at once and sit at his desk. He came down and took Hege's place, which was next to mine. I sat at the third desk from the front in the middle row, and Hege sat on my right, only now the teacher was there. So Hege began to read. She was one of the best at reading aloud, but now she read so quietly that the teacher had to ask her to speak up. Hege raised her voice, but after a moment it broke and she had to begin again. She glanced down at me several times, and once I waved discreetly back with my left index finger. When she'd finished reading the teacher began to clap, not for her delivery, but for the content of the essay, and so I clapped as well. As Hege made her way back to her desk I asked the teacher if we could watch her do the cha-cha-cha as well, but he said jocularly that that would have to wait for another time. Hege looked as if she were about to pull a face at me, but she didn't dare. Perhaps she was afraid I might suddenly snatch glory away from her by telling the class that it was I who'd gallantly stepped in to do her homework while she practised so intensely for a dancing competition. There could never be any question of that, as Hege had been most punctual in paying what had been agreed – I'd already got the two and a half kroner. But this didn't seem to put her mind at rest. She didn't realise just how often I helped classmates with their homework. It wasn't the first time I'd sat listening as an opus of mine was read to the class and, far from minding, I relished it. I was the Good Samaritan. I helped the whole class.

Hege was in the same set as me when we started grammar school and in the first year we had an amusing wager. Laila Nipen, one of our teachers, had won a load of money on the lottery and she'd spent it buying a brand new Fiat 500. I think I was the one who suggested that some of us boys might carry the tiny car through the double doors of the school entrance and set it down right in the middle of the assembly hall. Hege thought it was a great idea, but she didn't think we'd got the nerve. I saw my chance and suggested she swear a solemn oath to come on a romantic trip to the woods with me if Laila's Fiat made it to the assembly hall within the week. If it didn't, I'd do her maths homework for an entire month. A couple of days later the car was in the hall. The entire operation took just ten minutes, during a break when we knew there was a staff meeting. We even had the temerity to tie an outsized, light-blue ribbon round the little red car to make it look like a proper lottery prize. For its part, the school never found out who'd been responsible for that mischievous little prank, but Hege was now honour-bound to take a trip to the woods with me. She didn't try to overlook the obvious subtext in 'romantic'. Hege was no fool, she knew just how scheming I could be, and after all, I had helped to carry an entire car into the hall just for her sake. Anyway, I think she liked me. We found a secluded, unlocked shack. It was the first time I'd been with a naked girl. We weren't more than fourteen, but she was fully developed. I thought she was the loveliest thing I'd ever touched.

Now and then I used to help the teachers too. I was constantly feeding them amusing ideas for essay titles and other homework. A couple of times I offered to help the teacher mark our maths work. On other occasions I might ask for further, or more detailed, information about a subject the teacher had touched on in class. If we'd been learning about the Egyptians in a history lesson, I would exhort the teacher to tell the class about the Rosetta stone. Without this stone, scholars would never have been able to interpret hieroglyphics, I explained, and so we'd have known very little about how the ancient Egyptians thought. When the teacher told us about Copernicus, I asked if he could touch on Kepler and Newton too, because it's well known that not all Copernicus' suppositions were correct.

I was widely read by the time I was only eleven or twelve. At home we had both Aschehoug's and Salmonsen's encyclopaedias which came to forty-three volumes in all. According to motivation and mood, I had three different modes of approaching an encyclopaedia: I might look up articles on a particular subject, often related to something I'd been pondering for some time; I might sit for hours and dip into the encyclopaedia at random; or I might begin to study one entire volume from start to finish, like Aschehoug's volume 12 from *Kvam* to *Madeira* or Salmonsen's volume XVIII from *Nordland Boat* to *Pacific*. My mother had dozens of other interesting books in the living-room bookcases. I was especially keen on comprehensive works that covered all the knowledge on a particular subject, for example *The World of Art*, *The World of Music*, *The Human Body*, Francis Bull's *World Literary History*, Bull, Paasche, Winsnes and Hoem's *The History of Norwegian Literature* and Falk and

Torp's *Etymological Dictionary of the Norwegian and Danish Tongues*. When I was twelve, my mother bought Charlie Chaplin's *My Autobiography*, and despite its lack of objectivity, it too became a kind of encyclopaedia. My mother was always nagging me to remember to put the books back on the shelves, and one day she banned me from taking more than four books into my room at once. 'You can't read more than one book at a time, anyway,' she declared. She didn't seem to realise that often the whole point was to compare what was written about a particular thing in several different books. I don't think my mother had a very sharp eye for source criticism.

After we'd learnt about the prophets in religious instruction, I asked the teacher to look up the prophet Isaiah, chapter 7, verse 14. I wanted him to explain to the class the difference between a 'virgin' and a 'young woman'. Surely the teacher knew that the Hebrew word translated as 'virgin' in that verse actually only signified a 'young woman'? This was something I'd chanced on in Salmonsen's encyclopaedia. But, I went on, Matthew and Luke appeared not to have studied the underlying Hebrew text carefully enough. Perhaps they had contented themselves with the Greek translation, called the Septuagint, which I thought was such a funny name. *Septuaginta* was the Latin for 'seventy', and the first Greek translation of the Old Testament was so named because it was made by seventy learned Jews in seventy days. I elaborated on all of this.

The teacher didn't always welcome my contributions to his lessons, even though I took great care not to correct him when he said things that were factually wrong. When I ventured to attack the very dogma of the virgin birth by referring to what I considered was a translation error in the Septuagint, he was further constrained by church doctrine and the school's charter. He tried to hush me up, too, when

I pointed out something as innocent as the way Jesus' public ministry lasted three years in John's gospel, but only one year according to the other Evangelists.

When we were doing human biology I told the teacher that I thought his use of the word 'winkle' for a certain bodily member was utterly risible, at least in the context of propagation. I told him that the term 'winkle' had fallen completely out of fashionable use, especially in matters of sexuality. 'Which term do you think I should use instead?' he asked. The teacher was a sympathetic chap, a powerfully built man and almost six foot six into the bargain, but now he was completely at sea. 'I haven't a clue,' I replied. 'You'll just have to try to find something else. But do try to avoid Latin,' I said by way of a parting shot.

I never gave pieces of advice to the teacher during the class. My aim wasn't to demonstrate that I was cleverer than my classmates or even, from time to time, cleverer than the teacher. It was always in the schoolyard or on the way in and out of the classroom that I gave the teacher friendly tips. I didn't do it to make an impression on him, or to feign a greater preoccupation with school work than was really the case. The opposite was nearer the mark. I would sometimes pretend to be less interested than I was, which was much more fun. So did I do it out of pure, unalloyed benevolence? No, that wasn't true, either.

I'd regularly feed the teacher good bits of advice because I found it fascinating to watch his reaction. I enjoyed watching people perform. I enjoyed watching them disport themselves.

★

Each Saturday I'd listen to *Children's Hour*, and I wasn't alone. Every child in Norway listened to *Children's Hour*. In later life, I saw an official statistic that said that in the period 1950 to 1960, 98 per cent of all Norwegian children listened to *Children's Hour*. That must have been a very conservative estimate.

We lived in what social scientists call a homogenous culture. Everyone with any self-respect listened to *The Road to Agra*, *Karlson on the Roof* and *Little Lord Fauntleroy*. Everyone read the Bobsey Twins, Nancy Drew and the Famous Five books. We were brought up with Torbjørn Egner and Alf Prøysen. We also had a shared experience in the long weather forecasts from the Met. Office, the arid Stock Exchange prices, Saturday night from the Big Studio at Marienlyst, *Family Favourites*, that now dated mix called *Music and Good Motoring* and *Dickie Dick Dickens*. Every Norwegian of my age shares the same cultural background. We were like one big family.

Children's Hour was accompanied by a 50-øre bar of chocolate, a small bottle of fizzy orange and either a packet of alphabet biscuits, a small box of raisins or a bag of peanuts. On the rare occasions we got both raisins and peanuts, we mixed them. The Saturday treat was almost as standardised as school breakfast. For school breakfast the education authorities supplied milk, crispbread with cheese, and bread with liver pâté, fish paste and jam. It was during school breakfast that I would sometimes take soundings to find out what the others were given for *Children's Hour*. It appeared that everyone got exactly the same as me. I found it eerie to discover that there was some unseen parental conspiracy in operation. This was before I realised just how deep a homogenous culture could sit.

Sometimes we were given a krone so that we could go to the sweet shop and choose our own Saturday treat. Of course, this was far better than the usual mix of peanuts, raisins and alphabet biscuits. A krone would buy us ten mini chocolate bars, but with ten øre you could also get one jelly baby or two salt pastilles or one piece of chewing-gum or two five-øre chocolates or four fruit pastilles. So, for a full krone you could buy three mini chocolate bars, two jelly babies, two salt pastilles, one piece of chewing-gum, four five-øre chocolates and four fruit pastilles. Or you could buy a 25-øre bar of chocolate, a 25-øre sherbet lemon and, for example, two mini chocolate bars, two jelly babies and a piece of chewing gum. I was good at making my money go a long way. Sometimes I would also filch small change from my mother's coat pocket, when she was getting ready in the bathroom, or having an after-dinner nap, or late in the evening when she was sitting listening to *La Bohème*. Taking a small coin or two didn't give me a bad conscience, because I only did it when I hadn't used the phone for days. Four phone calls cost one krone – I was already a very businesslike little person. But for my mother's sake I was careful to avoid any jingling of keys or coins when I stuck my hand into her coat pocket. Metre Man often stood watching me, but he wouldn't tell. An extra krone or 50 øre made selecting the Saturday sweets much easier.

Not everyone had a state-of-the-art radio, but my mother and I did. We had just traded in an old Radionette for a brand new Tandberg Temptress. The set stood on a teak shelf in the living-room and banana plugs attached it to two loudspeakers. These gave far better sound quality than the cabinet radios. The shelf below the radio set and record player contained all of mother's records: an impressive number of old 78s, but also a lovely collection of modern LPs and singles. Once I'd bought my supply of sweets for *Children's Hour*, I'd perch on the Persian pouffe right up close to one of the loudspeakers and lay out all my sweets in one long row on top of the radio. If I had more sweets than my official means dictated, I'd make a secret little row of chocolates and jelly babies down on the record shelf as well. In such circumstances, I'd always consume the lower row first.

The grown-ups also bought themselves treats to go with their Saturday coffee. I'd made thorough investigations about this too during school breakfasts, and the impression I got concurred almost uncannily with what I'd observed in my own home. The grown-ups ate large 25-øre crystallised fruits, little liqueur chocolates, chocolate orange segments or slabs of dark chocolate. If visitors came in the morning, they'd have tea and fresh rolls with vegetable mayonnaise, and if it was an extra special occasion, they'd buy French sticks and make great open sandwiches with roast beef, prawn salad, ham and liver pâté.

My mother assumed I listened to *Children's Hour* because I thought it was fun. She didn't realise I was sitting there wrapped in my own thoughts. She didn't realise that I was sitting on the pouffe working out how *Children's Hour* might be vastly improved. If radio was claiming the attention of every Norwegian child for a whole hour each week, I thought the quality of the programme should be impeccable. I put together an entire raft of good programme ideas – with everything from listener competitions, jokes and ghost stories to sketches, animal tales, real-life stories, fairy tales and radio plays, all of which I'd written myself. I timed each piece and always kept within the sixty minutes. It was instructive. An impressive amount could be slotted into sixty minutes – it merely required an iota of critical faculty. That's something I've always possessed, but unfortunately the same couldn't be said of Lauritz Johnson. Even a man of Alf Prøysen's stature ought to have asked himself how many times we'd want to hear that he'd put a two-øre bit in his piggy-bank. Walt Disney had a critical faculty, he was divine, he had created his own universe. In fact, Walt Disney and I had several things in common. In the days before he'd created his own Disneyland, he had also been inspired by the Tivoli Gardens in Copenhagen. I worked out several great Donald Duck stories, intending to send them to Walt Disney, but I never got round to it.

I didn't send in my suggestions to the Norwegian Broadcasting Corporation, either. If I had, they would certainly have acted on them, but I didn't want to listen to an entire *Children's Hour* that I'd already worked out in my head. And so I kept all my sprightly ideas to myself. Not everyone is so restrained as that, as splendidly exemplified by the development of television.

When Norwegian television made its first official broadcast in 1960, I was visiting a neighbour and heard the Prime Minister's inaugural speech. Prime Minister Einar Gerhardsen pointed out that many people understandably feared that television would become a distracting intrusion into childhood and family life. They were worried, he said, that watching television would adversely affect children's homework and recreational activities in the fresh air and sunshine. 'The development of television will probably be similar to that of radio,' the Prime Minister declared. 'When something is new it's natural that people want to get as much of it as they can.' But Einar Gerhardsen thought this would right itself. Gradually we would learn to be choosy. 'We must get better at selecting things with special value,' he said, 'we must learn to switch off the programmes that don't interest us. Only then will television become really useful and enjoyable.' Gerhardsen hoped that television would become another tool for teaching and general education, and a further channel for disseminating knowledge throughout the country. He expected television to be a key to new values of heart and mind, and he emphasised that there ought to be strict quality controls on programmes for children and young people.

Einar Gerhardsen was an inveterate optimist. He was also a good man who fortunately never lived long enough to see how television as a medium degenerated. If Einar Gerhardsen had been alive today, he would have been able to flick his way through a rich flora of soap operas and fly-on-the-wall documentaries on a host of different channels. He would have witnessed just how keenly television companies compete for quality, especially as regards programmes watched by children and young people. He would have seen how clever we've become at selecting what is of special value.

I'd actually invited myself over to a neighbour who'd bought a television set. I wasn't shy about inviting myself – I was eight, after all. The summer holidays had just ended, and I was now in the Second Form. This new medium was something I had to be in on from the start.

This neighbour hadn't any children, that was what was so good about it, and I don't think he had a wife, either – at least I'd never seen him with a woman – but he did have a big Labrador called Waldemar. I made sure I got there early enough to play with Waldemar a bit before the first, official television broadcast began. My neighbour appreciated this. I asked if he thought dogs could think, and he was quite sure they could. He explained that he could tell by Waldemar's eyes if he was dreaming or if he was just asleep. He could read this from his tail as well. 'In that case, he only dreams about bones or dog biscuits,' I interjected, 'and maybe bitches as well, but I don't think a dog can dream a whole play. Dogs can't talk,' I pointed out, 'so I don't think they can have very strange dreams.' My neighbour believed Waldemar could clearly signal when he was hungry or when he wanted to relieve himself, nor was it hard to see when he was happy or sad or frightened. 'But he can't tell fairy tales,' I insisted. 'There isn't enough imagination in his head for it to overflow, and that's why he can't cry either.' My neighbour agreed with me there. He said he had to make sure he took Waldemar out for a walk so that he didn't pee on the living-room floor, but luckily he didn't have to worry that Waldemar might suddenly build a puppet theatre out of sofa cushions or start drawing Donald Duck cartoons on the walls. 'Dogs aren't as communicative as us,' he said, 'perhaps that's what you mean.' And that was exactly what I meant. I said: 'Even so, they may be just as happy.'

We weren't able to say more because now it was Einar Gerhardsen's turn. My neighbour and I shared a moment of national celebration. Waldemar padded out into the kitchen and occupied himself with something quite different.

The new medium had soon become a huge challenge. Within a year I'd managed to persuade my mother to buy a television set, and soon I was bubbling over with ideas for programmes. I didn't send any of them in, but I was constantly phoning up the television service telling them what I thought.

One of the programme ideas I'd come up with was to put ten people into an empty house. They were to be isolated from the outside world and not allowed to leave before they had created something totally new. It had to be something of lasting significance for people the world over. It might, for example, be a new and better declaration of human rights, or the world's most beautiful fairy tale, or a production of the world's funniest play. The participants were to have plenty of time – I think I reckoned on one hundred days. That's a long time. That's more than enough time. And when there are ten of you to fill the hundred days, it's really a thousand days, in fact almost three years. If the will is there, ten people can do quite a lot in a hundred days. One prerequisite was that the participants had to learn to work together. Each time they had anything important to announce to humanity, they could ring up TV head-quarters, and one of the well-known presenters would go to the house with a camera crew to hear what they were suggesting that was so important for mankind. At the time it wasn't normal to use twenty or thirty different cameras to make an entertainment programme. There weren't that many cameras in the whole of the television service – it was before we Norwegians had discovered North Sea oil. You were also supposed to have something to say before you appeared in front of a television camera. Not everyone did, but it was at least regarded as desirable. Even in those days there were programmes featuring meaningless gather-ings of people, and we were served up things like the annual school graduation trips to Copenhagen, but it would have been unthinkable to film a gathering or graduation trip that lasted a hundred days. It was a different age, a different culture, and perhaps even something as remote as a different civilisation. I don't say this in my own defence, but today's television culture was beyond the bounds of my conception. Soon I had a whole notebook full of good programme suggestions, but the idea that it would become possible to set new viewing records by making a television series hundreds of hours long about a gang of giggling girls and itchy-fingered youths, surpassed my wildest fantasy. It's unlikely that Caesar or Napoleon had sufficient imagination to envisage atomic weapons or cluster bombs, either. It can be wiser to leave certain notions for the future. There's no intrinsic merit in using up all the bright ideas at once.

★

I was much alone during my teenage years too. The older I got, the more alone I became, but I loved it. I enjoyed sitting on my own, thinking. Gradually, as I grew up, I concentrated more and more on working out various plots for books, films and the theatre.

As a legacy from my childhood and youth, I had notes for hundreds of stories. They were rough drafts of everything from fairy tales, novels and short stories to theatre and film scripts. I never made any attempt to flesh the material out, I don't think the thought ever occurred to me. How could I possibly choose which novel I should begin to write when I had a whole pile of narratives to select from?

I was incapable of writing a novel in any event, I've always been too restless for that. While thinking and making notes my inspiration was of such intensity that my own chain of thought was constantly being interrupted as new ideas presented themselves, often much better ones than those I'd been working on in the first place. Novelists have a special talent for slogging away at the same story for long periods, often for several years. For me this is too inactive, too distracted and preoccupied.

Even if I'd mastered the mental inertia for writing a novel, I wouldn't have bothered to do it. I should have lacked the motivation to write the book once the idea had been born and had taken its place in notebook or ring-binder. The most important thing for me was to gather and earmark the greatest number of ideas, or what I later called subjects and synopses. Perhaps I may be compared to a hunter who loves hunting rare game, but who doesn't necessarily want to take part in cutting up and cooking the carcase, and subsequently, eating the meat. He could be a vegetarian. There's no contradiction in being a crack shot and a vegetarian at the same time – for dietary reasons, for instance. Similarly, there are many sports fishermen who don't like fish. But they still spend hours casting their lines and if they get a big fish, immediately give it away to friends or some chance passer-by. The most elite sports fishermen go one step further: they cast off and reel the fish in, only to return it to the water moments later. Good God, you don't stand there fishing all day just to save a little money on the housekeeping! The whole point of this august catch-and-release fishing is that the consumer, or utility, element is completely absent. One fishes because it's a balm. Fishing is a game of finesse, a noble art. This analogy puts me in mind of Ernst Jünger who wrote in one of his wartime diaries that one shouldn't grieve over a thought that gets away. It's like a fish that gets off the hook and swims down into the depths again, only to return one day even bigger . . . If, on the other hand, one lands the fish, guts it and chucks it into a plastic bucket, any further development of the fish has clearly been curtailed. Precisely the same can be said of the idea behind a novel once it is written out and set in more or less successful aspic, or even published. Perhaps the world of culture is characterised by too much catch and too little release.

There's another reason why I never wanted to write a novel, or start 'writing', as people often say. I considered it far too affected. Ever since I was a boy, I've been as scared of being affected as I was that my father might begin expressing gooey sentiments in that tunnel of love. If there was one thing I really hated as a child, it was being patted on the head or chucked under the chin. I found it unnatural, I didn't know how to respond to such advances.

This doesn't mean that I consider affectation a bad characteristic – not a bit of it – I love affected people, they have always amused me immensely. The vain are only eclipsed in my estimation by pure *poseurs* or those who are in love with themselves. Such people are even more fun to observe than the ones who are only moderately self-centred. I've always been able to pick out the most inflated characters in a crowded room. They are easy to observe, it's not hard to notice the peacock once its fan is spread. I find it more amusing to talk to the slightly vainglorious than to converse with people whose inflated egos are partly or wholly concealed by a cultivated interest in others. The vain always do their utmost to be as funny and entertaining as possible. They aren't lazy. They usually pull out all the stops.

Unfortunately, I'm congenitally bereft of vanity myself. It must be dull for the people about me, but it's something I've had to learn to live with. I would never have permitted myself to pull out all the stops. This is doubtless a mean attitude to life, I admit as much, but I've never allowed myself to dance to another's tune. I'm not denying I'm clever, but I couldn't have stood the thought of someone telling me so.

I would never have managed to do anything as pretentious as write, publish and present some novel or collection of short stories, thereafter to clamber up on to a pedestal and take my applause. And another thing: writing novels has become all too commonplace. Only the naïve write novels. One day it will be as common to write novels as it once was to read them.

Watching *Limelight* with my mother really brought home to me the brevity of life. I realised that in a little while I would die and leave everything behind. Unlike vain people, I had the ability to think this thought right through. I had no difficulty in picturing full theatres and cinemas long after I myself was gone. Not everyone can do that. Many are so intoxicated with sensual impressions that they're not able to grasp that there's a world out there. And therefore they're not able to comprehend the opposite either – they don't understand that one day the world will end. We, however, are only a few missing heartbeats away from being divorced from humanity for ever.

I've never tried to embellish what I am by showing off to others or posing in front of the mirror. I'm only on this planet for a brief visit. It's largely because of this that I've found it refreshing to talk to vain people.

Speaking to little children or watching a comedy by Holberg or Molière can have a particularly cleansing effect on the mind. In a similar way it's been a benison to meet the conceited. They are just as innocent as small children, and it is precisely this trust that I've caught myself envying. They live as if something can be achieved, as if something is up for grabs. But we are dust. So there's no point in making a fuss. Or as Mephistopheles says as Faust dies: *What matters our creative endless toil, when at a snatch oblivion ends the coil.*

★

My mother died just before Christmas 1970, while I was in my Sixth-Form year. Her illness came on quite suddenly. She was sick for only a short while, a month at home attending an Out Patients' clinic and then a few weeks in hospital.

My father and mother were completely reconciled in the weeks before she died, even before she was admitted to hospital. My father told me he'd wrecked my mother's life, and she said exactly the same about him, she said she'd ruined his life. And so they continued their lamentations and reproaches right up to the last. The difference was that they no longer blamed each other, now they only blamed themselves. The sum total of all this woe added up to much the same. It wasn't a matter of any great concern to me if my mother and father tortured each other or if they merely tortured themselves.

It was a fine funeral. My father made a long speech about what a wonderful person mother had been. He also went into what he termed 'the great fall from grace' in their lives. During recent days they'd managed to find their way back to one another, they'd forgiven each other's shortcomings, he said. And so they'd managed to fulfil the vow they'd once made before the priest. They had had their better days and their worse days. But they'd also managed to love one another until death parted them.

There wasn't a shred of dissimulation in my father's eulogy, he really did love mother in the weeks before she died. To me it had seemed rather late in the day and I felt he might have kept away for the few weeks she had left. Perhaps he loved her even more in the days immediately after her death. He didn't do it just to gain attention.

The idea was that I should say a few words by her coffin too, but I couldn't do it. I was really broken-hearted. I think I mourned her more than father, and that was why I couldn't say anything, it wasn't the moment for witticisms. If I hadn't cared so much about my mother's death, I should certainly have made a moving speech. I didn't realise it would affect me so deeply. I simply rose from my pew and walked to the coffin with a wreath of forget-me-nots. I nodded to my father and the priest, and father and the priest nodded back. As I stepped down to return to my seat, I saw that the little man in his green felt hat was pacing up and down in the aisle thrashing the air with his thin cane. He was irate.

I was over eighteen, and my father thought I should go on living in the flat despite mother's death. For some time afterwards we continued to see each other once a week. Early the following spring we decided that once a month was enough. We had outgrown skating heats and ski-jumping and all that. There were to be no more rides through the tunnel of love. Father lived to be over eighty.

In the weeks following my mother's death I remember thinking: mother can't see me any more. Who will see me now?

Maria

I didn't forget my mother, she would never be forgotten, but I liked having the flat to myself. Few people of my age had a flat of their own.

For a while I had no one to accompany me to the theatre or cinema, and that was something I missed, but soon I began to invite girls out. I didn't feel shy about it, I had no trouble in going up to a strange girl in the schoolyard and asking her out to a film or a theatre. Sometimes I met girls on the bus or in the shops, or in the centre of town. I felt it was better to ask a stranger out than to approach one of girls in my class. Asking a girl in my class could easily be misunderstood and, in addition, it required a certain amount of following up. Even though I didn't know the girl I was inviting out, her appearance always gave me some clue as to what she was like, and I could take a guess at how old she was, too.

It was easy to get talking to girls, and I was rarely turned down. They laughed, but from the manner in which I put the question, they didn't think it the slightest bit odd that I should ask them out, even though we'd never spoken before. I asked in a way that gave them the feeling of being chosen. And they had been, too. I didn't invite out every girl I saw.

The girls liked the fact that I had my own flat. One by one I brought them home for cheese and wine or om-elettes and lager. Sometimes they stayed the night, and only rarely the same girl twice. If I allowed the same girl to visit several times, it started to engender a sort of frustration about not being invited even more often. Occasionally, demands were made that I wasn't in a position to fulfil, and then I had to explain. I could have skipped the explanation, but I've always had a facility for making myself understood.

No one resented being invited to just one play, one evening out, one overnight stay. The problems only began after four or six such visits. It was a paradox. A girl with whom I'd spent a night was usually content with the fun she'd had. She didn't rush out into town and begin to prattle about it either. Most of them thought a one-night stand with a stranger a bit embarrassing. But as soon as their visits approached double figures, they began to complain, began to talk to girlfriends about it and to take it virtually for granted that the number of sleep overs would run into three and four figures.

I've never pulled the wool over girls' eyes. I never promised them supper before we'd been to the cinema or theatre, I never promised them a bed before we'd finished the meal, and I never held out any expectations of a return visit. I could be generous with my compliments, because I really did value such female company, but I never gave the impression that I wanted, or was even in a position, to commit myself for a longer period. In order to avoid mis-understandings I might stress, while lending a girl a towel, a toothbrush or in certain cases my mother's old dressing-gown, that even though it was nice to entertain someone for the night, she mustn't read more into it than that – a pleasant interlude. If I was especially fond of the girl, perhaps more fond of her than all the others put together, I felt it my sacred duty to make clear that I wasn't look-ing for any commitments. This made an impression, none of them rushed for the door. It seemed that plain speak-ing only made an overnight stay all the more exciting.

You often set more store by things you don't expect to be repeated, than those you believe will go on *ad infinitum*.

It was fun having a succession of girls over for visits, because each was interested in something different. A few went to the bookshelf and pulled out particular books that interested them. A girl called Irene sat flicking through *The World of Art*, and another called Randi began reading aloud from Karl Evang's book on sexual enlightenment. I'd dipped into it when I was little, but I considered it rather dated now. One of the girls immediately seated herself at the green piano and gave a faltering performance of one of Chopin's nocturnes – she was called Ranveig, I think – while Turid improvised tunes from the musical *Hair* by strumming some basic chords. At least fifty per cent of them just wanted to put on a record as soon as they entered the living-room. I had Joan Baez, Janis Joplin, Simon & Garfunkel and Peter, Paul & Mary. One blue-eyed blonde insisted that we listen to Karius and Baktus as well, but no one had yet shown any interest in Tchaikovsky or Puccini. The first time this happened was when, quite by chance, I met Hege again, sometime towards the end of May.

Hege had completed the Sixth Form college course in music, and when she came home after we'd been to the cinema to see *The Graduate*, she immediately went to the piano and played the whole of Rachmaninov's piano concerto no. 2 in C Minor. The concert lasted over half an hour and, for a brief moment, before she'd got far into the Adagio, I was convinced I was in love with her. But as soon as she began the concluding Allegro, I realised it was the music that had captivated me and not the pianist. As we went into the bedroom, she had fits of laughter when I reminded her of the theft of a red Fiat and the subsequent romance in a shed. Now we were adults, we hadn't seen each other since grammar school days.

Hege stayed at my place for three nights, but when she realised that we weren't proper lovers, she left on the fourth day and never got in touch again. I didn't find it hard to see her point of view. We'd known each other since we were children, and were almost too close to play at adult games just for the sake of it.

I believe Metre Man felt as I did, because he was particularly grouchy during the three days Hege was in the flat. He rushed about the living-room and kitchen and drilled with his bamboo cane right in front of her eyes. It was a mystery to me that she couldn't see him.

Lots of girls wanted to go out on to the veranda. My mother had always had a nice display in her window-boxes, and I couldn't bring myself to leave them untended that first spring after her death. I'd dug out and thrown away everything that was in the boxes from the previous year and then filled them to the brim with compost and planted a mass of bulbs. The result was surprisingly good. That spring the boxes on the veranda were bursting with lilies, crocuses and tulips as never before, and many of the girls showed how impressed they were with my green fingers. When the weather was fine we sometimes sat on the veranda looking out across the city with a glass of Martini or Dubonnet in our hands.

I had, naturally, to explain how I came to live alone, and as a consequence I showed some of them my mother's wardrobe. They were often allowed to take away a dress they fancied, or a suit or a coat. First, they had to try them on to see if they fitted; every time it was like a little fashion show. Then, just for fun, I might magic up a pair of gloves, a shawl or an elegant evening handbag just as they were about to leave. I was especially fond of the young woman who inherited the Persian lambskin coat. Her name was Therese and tears welled in her eyes as I folded the fleece up and slipped it into a large paper bag. But I don't think it was mere gratitude for the coat that moved her so much. I believe she saw the gift as part of some courtship ritual, or at any rate some deeply felt declaration of love, resonating with overtones and undertones and so, yet again, I had to explain myself. I told my father I'd given all the clothes to the Salvation Army, and he accepted this without demur – perhaps he'd forgotten the Persian lambskin coat – but it was the girls who'd helped themselves to most of her wardrobe, and some of them also made themselves useful by sorting out the things which just needed throwing away. It was six months before all of mother's clothes were out of the flat.

Occasionally someone I'd spent the night with would look the other way when we met in the street, but there were so many girls in Oslo in those days that it never caused any recruitment problem. In the early seventies spending a night with someone was no big deal. I remember thinking that I'd been born at the right time. For instance, it wouldn't have been such fun for a man of my age to have had his own flat twenty years earlier.

I was on nodding terms with many girls in the city even before I'd left Sixth Form college, but I'd never yet been in love. I felt too adult for that, I felt I was far too mature for the girls I associated with. It was here that a certain dualism was developing. I certainly didn't feel too adult for their bodies. But a woman isn't merely a body, and clearly a man isn't either. I was convinced that one day I'd meet a woman whom I could love with both body and soul. Perhaps that was the reason I began to go off on long hikes by myself. One day I'd find her and, if she was like me, it wouldn't be at a discotheque or in some youth group. A skiing hut was much more likely. And, in fact, I did meet her at Ullevålseter, but that wasn't until the middle of June.

★

At nursery school I'd enjoyed sitting in a corner watching all the children playing. Now the children were older, almost grown-up. It wasn't so thrilling to watch big children's games, or at least not the one called celebrating the end of school exams. I had a preference for pre- rather than post-school activities. For some weeks it was harder to find theatre companions and female visitors. There was too much going on in town.

Almost every day I set out on long walks in the forests round the northern suburbs of Oslo. I took the train to Finse and roamed the Hardanger plateau too, and I walked down Aurlandsdalen and got the train home from Flåm. I loved travelling by train, I enjoyed studying the people on it, and I found it hugely satisfying to let my mind wander as I moved through the landscape. School was over, in a few weeks I'd have certificates to say I'd passed with distinction in all subjects except gymnastics. I had nothing else to do but go walking and ride the train. My father was to pay me my allowance right up until 15 September.

When I was out mooching around on my own, I always took a notebook and pencil with me. I was particularly fond of turning things over in my mind as I walked. I thought all the time, but I found it easier to give free rein to my imagination while I was outdoors and moving, than sitting in a chair at home in the flat. Schiller pointed out that when man plays he is free, for then he follows his own rules. He had a point, but the thing could just as easily be turned the other way round: it was easier to play with thoughts and ideas when I was roaming at will on the Hardanger plateau than pacing about hour after hour between four walls, like some dormitory town detainee. And there was another thing: Metre Man kept to the flat by and large. He would occasionally appear in town, but it was very seldom that he turned up in the forest or on the Hardanger plateau.

My thoughts were fresher and bolder when I was walking, and new subjects and synopses streamed into my mind. At home I had large catalogues and indexes of my collection of plots for short stories, novels, plays and films. I'd typed up my best ideas before filing the pages away in a ring-binder. Once completed, I hardly ever took a synopsis out and looked at it again.

The notion of filling out any of my ideas still hadn't occurred to me. Hatching out tightly worked plots was only a hobby, little more than a weakness or an idiosyncrasy. Just as some people collect coins or stamps, I collected my own thoughts and ideas.

Once, one of the girls began flicking through one of my binders. She'd taken it off the shelf in my work-room and began reading it aloud. She didn't get invited to spend the night, omelettes and lager was enough. From then on I kept all the binders and indexes securely locked in two solid cupboards beneath the bookshelves in the living-room.

As I walked through Aurlandsdalen, an idea came to me. It was a completely novel one, and was linked to the fact that I'd just got to know a young author at Club 7. He was only four or five years older than me. I'd treated him to a bottle of wine, and we'd spent the whole evening talking in that Mecca of avant-garde pop music. Despite his tough, John Lennon glasses, his profusion of hair and beard and a passably shabby corduroy suit, he was fairly inane, but at least he wasn't as immature as my contemporaries, celebrating their exams. I pulled out some notes I'd written earlier in the day, three or four closely written pages comprising the detailed plot of a novel. I let him skim through it, and he was extremely impressed. He glanced up at me with an envious look, then heaped inordinate praise on what I'd shown him. It didn't surprise me. I knew I'd shown him a brilliant idea for a novel, but I took no pleasure in being praised, not by such a young and inexperienced author anyway. That wasn't why I'd shown him my notes. 'If you pay for the wine, I'll give you those notes,' I said. He just gawped. 'You're an author, after all,' I pointed out. 'I promise never to say where you got the idea from, but you must pay for the wine and give me fifty kroner.' So he refunded me the money I'd laid out on the wine, and a hundred kroner on top. At Club 7 you had to pay for a bottle of wine before it was opened. Just as I was taking the money, I saw Metre Man on the premises. He was strutting irritably amongst the café tables, then he suddenly turned towards our table and shook his bamboo cane at me.

Today that young man with the John Lennon glasses is one of the country's leading authors, and he turned fifty not long ago. I was to meet him on many subsequent occasions and now I take ten per cent of everything he earns from his books. But only he and I know that.

In Aurlandsdalen I stood for a long time in front of a large pothole called 'Little Hell', and it was here it struck me for the first time that all those ideas of mine might actually provide me with a living after all. I was in possession of a commodity with which certain people weren't over-endowed. I wasn't vain and had no wish to be famous, but I was short of money and I didn't plan on getting a summer job. Nor would I have anything to live on after 15 September. My father had made it crystal clear that after that date the tap would be turned firmly off. But, as he said, I would probably go on to study, and every student got a student loan. What my father didn't realise was that I couldn't possibly live on such a thing anyway. My female visitors alone broke any budget that the State Educational Loan Fund might advance. In addition, if I was short of money my freedom of movement was curtailed. This was an idea I didn't like at all.

That sudden inspiration touched me only lightly, the same way all impulses settled on my consciousness. The reason I mention it here is merely to show that I can recall the exact time and place where the idea first was born. It was as I stood staring down into Little Hell. I remember thinking it was a good idea, it was a meta-idea, an idea that took a firm grasp of all the other ideas I'd had and seemed to slot them into place.

Looking back now, it's rather tempting to regard that hike through Aurlandsdalen as my pact with the devil.

While I was out walking in the countryside, I often thought of all the years that had gone by. Something was over, and something new was just about to begin. I had to find myself a respectable, but anonymous, place in society.

I was already sometimes unable to distinguish between recalled reality and recalled fantasy. This was the result of my special talent for harbouring vivid memories of my imaginary world while at the same time having a somewhat hazy recollection of real life. It could scare me, it could make me a trifle nervous, but it is over-simplistic to conclude that I had a traumatic childhood and that I therefore repressed it. My mother thought I had an unhappy childhood – she knew no better. Personally, I regarded my childhood as particularly rich.

I remember how I once flew over the city. I looked down on all the houses and was free to choose where to land and which living-rooms and bedrooms to peep into. Looking through the windows, I could see how a wide cross-section of people lived, and there was no secret I couldn't share. I witnessed everything from various forms of domestic disturbance to the most bizarre sexual deviations. It was like studying monkeys in a cage, and sometimes I felt ashamed of my own species. Once I saw a man and a woman having sex on a large, deep-pile rug while a girl of two or three sat watching from the sofa. I thought it unnatural. Another time I watched a man who was lying on a big double bed romping with two women at once. It didn't arouse my moral indignation, but there were many other observations that could leave me shaken. On one occasion, and unable to intervene, I witnessed a vicious fight over money. I wasn't quite sure, but it looked rather like one man was left for dead inside the flat after the other had made off.

These are obviously remembered fantasy, but I learnt from such fantasies. They were often full of insight. Much of the material for the many detective novels I later inspired was gathered from these mental journeys. Usually, a detective novel has a plot that can be condensed into a single page. The author's skill is simply to keep this kernel of factual information back. The detective must spend time – and use cunning – to arrive at the solution. That's what the readers like. Piece by piece, the investigator gets a better idea of what has actually happened. He must also be decoyed up blind alleys, but as the picture gradually becomes clearer and more complete, the readers feel clever, they believe that they have helped to solve the case themselves.

I learnt from dreams as well. A dream could be like an open book. At the time I had two or three recurrent dream landscapes, as well as a few dream characters who manifested themselves at regular intervals. I was convinced they weren't just a reflex to stimuli from the external world; far from it, they represented something new, they were genuine new experiences from which I learnt and which have moulded me into the man I am today. But where did the dreams come from? I couldn't work out if all my dreams and mental journeys were the fruits of specially sensitive antennae attuned to things that came from outside, or if I had some sonar of the soul that was able to detect layer upon layer of secrets from a bottomless well within me.

I no longer dreamt of the little man with the cane, though I wouldn't have minded meeting him in a sleeping dream. It would have been far preferable to dream about him than have him roaming around the flat the whole time.

I made even more spectacular mental journeys, too. I went to the moon, for example, long before Armstrong and Aldrin. I remember once standing on the surface of the moon and looking up at the earth. High up there were all the people. It has since become a cliché, but years before Armstrong made that giant leap for mankind, I found myself on the moon discovering for the first time how tragi-comic all wars and national boundaries were. I was possibly twelve when I made that journey of the mind. Ever since then, I've had a heightened sense of all the trivialities with which people pack their lives. Praise and punishment, fame and honour seemed even more farcical.

Some of my mental travels took me even further into space. I once went on a time-machine trip and arrived back on earth before there was any life here. I moved over the face of the waters, and the earth lay like a bud that's ready to burst, because I knew that life on earth would begin soon. That was about five billion years before Gerhardsen's first government.

Or I could rove about on mental wings to various places in the city, like the fly-loft in a theatre where I could sit high up, just beneath the roof, and gaze down at all the actors. On one occasion the little man was seated on a lighting batten only five feet away from me. He glanced furtively at me with a world-weary face and said in a thick voice: *So you're here as well, are you? Can't I ever do anything on my own?* That was a bit rich coming from *him*.

I kept on getting new ideas. Sometimes they breathed down my neck, fluttered like butterflies in my stomach, or ached like open wounds. I bled stories and narratives, my brain effervesced with novel concepts. It was as if this fever-red lava welled up from the hot crater within me.

Relieving the pressure of my thoughts was a constant necessity, almost ceaselessly having to go somewhere where I could sit discreetly with a pencil and paper and let them all out. My excretions might consist of long conversations between two or more voices in my head, and frequently on specific ontological, epistemological or aesthetic subjects. One voice might say: *It is perfectly clear to me that the human being has an eternal soul, which only inhabits a body of flesh and blood for a short while.* The other voice might answer: *No, no. Man is an animal just like any other. What you term the soul is inextricably linked to a brain, and the brain is ephemeral. Or, as the Buddha said on his deathbed: All that is composite is transitory.*

Such dialogues could soon run to dozens of sheets of A4 paper, but it always felt good to get them out of my head. And yet, no sooner had I transferred them to paper, than I was full of voices again and had to relieve myself once more.

The dialogues I spewed out might just as easily be of a thoroughly mundane nature. One voice might say: *So there you are. Couldn't you at least have phoned to say you'd be late?* And the other voice would answer: *I told you the meeting might last a long time.* Then the first voice again: *You don't mean to say you've been sitting in a meeting all this time? It's almost midday!* And so the row would begin.

I never worked out in advance what such introductory exchanges presaged. Indeed, it was to avoid thinking about it that I willingly sat down and wrote the entire altercation out, so as to get it out of my system. The only way to get relief from an over-active mind was to fix its impulses in writing.

Occasionally I would bathe my brain in alcohol and, when I did, the spirit would flow back out again as stories; it was as if the liquid evaporated and got distilled as pure intellect. Though alcohol had a very stimulating effect on my imagination, it also dampened my angst about it too. It both primed the engine within me and gave me strength to endure its workings. I might have a shoal of thoughts in my head, but after a few drinks I was man enough to corner them all.

When I woke up in the morning I couldn't always remember what I'd been writing or making notes about the evening before, or at least, the very last thing I'd scribbled on the writing pad after a couple of bottles of wine. Then, it could be exciting to sling on a dressing gown and saunter into my work-room just to cast a glance over my desk. It wasn't inconceivable that something interesting might be lying there and, if I found a sheaf of notes I had no recollection of writing, it was almost like receiving a mysterious document that had come to me via automatic writing.

Perhaps one driving force behind my imagination and my periodic drinking was that thing I was always trying to forget, but which I couldn't really remember either. Why did I expend so much energy forgetting something that I couldn't even recollect?

★

Only the countryside and visits from girls could provide me with brief interludes of a kind of intellectual peace.

I was a natural mystic even before I began Sixth Form college. I saw the world as a thing dreamlike and bewitched. I wrote in my diary: *I've seen through almost everything. The only thing I am unable to fathom is the world itself. It is too vast. It is too impenetrable. I've long since given up as far as that's concerned. It's the only thing that stands in the way of a feeling of total insight.*

I was also a romantic. I could never have contemplated telling a girl I loved her if it wasn't true. Perhaps that was why I kept inviting all those girls. I realised that one day I might become a faithful lover. As far as I was concerned, I'd have been able to spend the rest of my life in a little cabin in the woods together with the girl I really loved. I just had to find her first. While I was out walking I was convinced she could turn up at any moment. Perhaps she'd be there on the path round the next bend, I really thought it was possible. It's no exaggeration. I hadn't the slightest doubt she existed.

★

That June day I'd walked to Ullevålseter from another skiing hut. There was virtually no one hiking in the forests surrounding Oslo on a hot summer afternoon; perhaps that was why it held such a special air of anticipation. For a large portion of the journey I hadn't met a soul, and that increased the chance that she might suddenly come walking towards me. If the forest had been packed with people it would have been harder for us to notice each other, and we certainly wouldn't have stopped to chat.

I went into the café and bought a waffle and a cup of hot blackcurrant before going out to rest on the grass. On a bench a little way off sat a girl with dark curls. She was wearing blue jeans and a red jumper and we were the only two people at Ullevålseter. She was sipping something too, but after a while she got up and came sauntering over towards me. For a moment I was afraid she was one of the girls who'd slept over at my place – a number had been brunettes, some with curly hair, and it wasn't easy to remember them all. But the woman who stood before me now must have been quite a bit older, she might have been eight or ten years their senior. A girl my age would never have taken such an unself-conscious initiative. She sat down on the grass and said her name was Maria. She was Swedish by the sound of her voice, and I'd never been with a Swedish girl before. I was convinced that Maria was the person I'd been searching for over the past few months. It had to be us, there was no one else here. It would have been too much of a coincidence to meet at Ullevålseter on a hot June afternoon unless we were meant for each other.

After only a few minutes' casual conversation we were speaking quite freely and easily and felt almost like old acquaintances. She was twenty-nine and had just finished a doctorate in the history of art at Oslo University. Prior to that she'd studied Renaissance art in Italy. She lived on the university campus, and this was another auspicious novelty. The girls I'd previously met always had to come back to my place because they lived with large families of parents and younger siblings. Maria had been born in Sweden, but her parents now lived in Germany.

She was quite unique, but the better I got to know Maria, the more I thought that we had much in common. She was charming, engaging and playful all at once. But she had something of my own talent for making swift associations and imaginative leaps. She possessed a refined, cognitive imagination and was the same cornucopia of thoughts, attitudes and ideas as me. She was sensitive and easily hurt, but she could also be inconsiderate and uncouth. Maria was the first person I'd met for whom I had a genuine feeling and with whom I was able and willing to communicate. It was as if we were a split soul: I was Animus, and she was Anima.

I fell deeply in love for the first time in my life, and I didn't experience the love itself as at all superficial. I'd known many girls, a great many in fact. It wasn't out of any lack of experience that I fell so heavily for Maria. I felt I'd built a solid foundation on which to start a serious relationship.

Even as we sat out on the grass at Ullevålseter, I began to tell Maria stories. It was as if she could see from my eyes that I was full of stories, as if she knew she could simply tease them out of me. She always knew which were made up and which were real. Maria understood irony and meta-irony – so essential for true communication.

I told a small selection of my best stories, and Maria not only sat and listened, but she commented, asked questions and made various intelligent suggestions. Nevertheless, she always agreed with my endings, and not out of politeness either, but because she realised she couldn't bring them to a better conclusion herself. Had I said something foolish or inconsistent, she would have been the first to pull me up. But I didn't say anything foolish or inconsistent, everything I told Maria that afternoon was well thought through. And she knew it. Maria was an adult.

We began to walk down towards Lake Sognsvann. It felt superfluous to suggest that we spend the rest of the afternoon and evening together. We fizzed, we sparkled, it was as if we were bathing in champagne froth.

However, even on that first meeting I believe I must have realised that Maria's affinity to me included an unwillingness to rush into giving any kind of guarantees for the immediate future. For the first time I was prepared to tell a girl that she might come to occupy the role of the woman in my life, but I couldn't tell if Maria was willing to allow me to play such an important role in hers.

Just before we got down to the lake it began to rain. The air was sultry. We sought shelter in the bushes beneath some huge, overhanging boughs not far from the path. I put my arms about her, and she embraced me. She loosened my belt, and we took off each other's jeans. It was only after we'd begun to caress that I asked her if she was on the pill. She smiled roguishly, but shook her head. 'Why not?' I asked. She laughed. 'You're looking at it all back to front,' she replied. I was confused. It was the first time I'd been with a girl I didn't understand. She said: 'I'm not on the pill because I'm quite happy to have a baby.' I said she was mad.

When she'd had her pleasure, I ejaculated into the bilberry bushes. Maria laughed again. She was ten years older than the other girls I'd been with. She didn't make a big thing of the fact that I'd come in the bushes because she wasn't on the pill. And I'm sure Metre Man didn't either. He just stood out in the rain under his damp felt hat, thrashing at the bushes with his spindly cane.

We were together every day in the weeks that followed. For the first time I knew someone who I felt was my equal. I'd had a good time with girls before, but I was never sorry to see them go the next morning. I'd learnt to abhor breakfast soppiness. Many of my girlfriends viewed breakfast as a sort of prelude, I saw it as a finale. But I would have missed Maria if she'd suddenly decided to leave after breakfast. But because we were so alike, I thought she might vanish from me at any moment. I also realised that Maria had a low threshold for the kind of company she could tolerate in preference to her own. I still satisfied that threshold.

I was always drunk with new ideas after we'd been

together. Maria knew it. She would ask me to tell her what I was thinking, and I would narrate a story, usually a completely new story I'd invented off the top of my head. Sometimes I had the impression that she just went to bed with me because she knew it was the surest way to hear yet another enthralling tale. I wouldn't have minded that arrangement provided it had been an explicit one. I hadn't done anything blameworthy to the girls I'd been with, and Maria couldn't be accused of doing anything unjust to me. We were the same. We shared the same shameless erotic devotion, the same cynical tenderness. We feasted upon one another, the question was merely which one of us would leave the table first.

One evening we went to the opera and saw *Madame Butterfly*. The fact that Maria liked Puccini too gave me great pleasure. Years had passed, but it was as if things had come full circle and we were again at the opera watching *Madam Butterfly*, the only difference was that now no one tried to refuse us a glass of Cinzano between the first and second acts. Pinkerton's betrayal was just as callous as before, he broke the heart of the delicate girl from Nagasaki, but neither Puccini nor his librettists could have guessed that only a few years later the Americans would be back to crush the whole of Nagasaki. We saw it at the height of the Vietnam war, and after the performance we went to a bar in Stortorget and talked about the many thousands of Pinkertons in Saigon – and the even greater number of butterflies.

★

I wasn't surprised when Maria appeared one day at the end of August and said that our relationship had to end. It merely saddened me. I felt stupid. I felt just as awkward as the girls who'd believed that four or six nights together could form the basis of a lasting relationship.

The reason I wasn't taken aback by Maria's sudden announcement was that several times recently she'd spoken about being frightened of me. She'd begun to be frightened of looking into my eyes, she told me on one occasion. When I asked why, she turned away and said that all the stories I recounted made her apprehensive, she was scared of what she called my overweening imagination. I was amazed by her jitteriness. Later she explained that she still loved hearing me narrate, and that it wasn't the stories themselves that worried her, but that, in the long run, she didn't know if she could sustain an intimate relationship with someone who inhabited his own world more than the real one. I'd been rash enough to tell her about the little man with the bamboo cane as well, and a couple of times I'd pointed him out in the room. Honesty isn't always the best policy.

Now she told me that she'd applied for a job in Stockholm. It was a curator's post at one of the big museums.

We continued seeing each other after this, but only once or twice a week. We remained good friends, there was never any ill-feeling between us. I remembered how I'd continued on good terms with the girls who'd spent the night with me.

We went to the cinema and theatre together, and occasionally we'd go for long walks in the forests around Oslo. I told her several stories, though now only when she asked for them, but we no longer lay together in the bilberry bushes. We didn't share Maria's bed at the campus either. The bilberries were ripe now. I missed her body.

One warm summer's evening when we'd thrown ourselves down on the manicured landscape in front of Frognerseter's café and restaurant, I spent several hours relating a long story about a chess game with living pieces.

This was after we'd spoken to a Scots couple who'd pointed across Oslofjord and remarked how like Scotland Norway was. I made the story up as I went along; it had a large cast of characters, and Maria was particularly impressed by the way I managed to think up all the Scottish names. The basic outlines of the story were these:

Lord Hamilton had been widowed early in life and lived on a large estate in the Scottish Highlands. From his childhood he'd been an ardent chess player and, as he also loved being out in the sumptuous garden behind his stately home, he'd built a large, outdoor chess board in the open space between an intricate maze of clipped hedges and a fine fish-pond. The chess board itself consisted of sixty-four black and white marble slabs two metres square, and the chessmen, which were of carved wood, were between two and three feet high depending on the value and rank of the individual piece. The servants of the house might stand at the windows and watch their master moving about the marble slabs and shifting the huge chessmen late on summer evenings. He sometimes seated himself in a garden chair, and then it could be an hour before he rose to make the next move.

The laird had a loud bell that he rang when he wanted his butler to bring him a tray of whisky and water, and sometimes the butler would ask him if he wasn't coming indoors soon. He was solicitous for his master's health and, at the back of his mind, there was probably also the fear that Lord Hamilton's sorrow at the loss of his wife, combined with his passionate love of chess, might one day turn his brain. This nascent anxiety was in no way diminished when one evening the laird told him to stand on the chessboard and pretend to be the black knight, as the real black knight had gone in for repair after a violent thunderstorm. For almost two hours the butler stood on the chessboard, and only occasionally in the course of the game did the laird come out on to the marble slabs and push him two squares forward and one to the side, or one square back and two to the side. When, finally, he was taken by a white bishop and could at last return to the house – though many hours before the game itself was over – he was cold and cross, but naturally most relieved as well.

When the laird moved the black and white chessmen, it was impossible to tell if he favoured one side or the other in the game. This was because he was in fact playing both sides as well as he could, he was playing both for and against himself, so he both won and lost every game, unless it ended in a stalemate. But with growing frequency he would also carry all the chessmen off the board and place them on the great lawn. Then, for hours, he would sit staring out over the marble squares. His employees said that in this state he could see the chessmen on the board even though they weren't there, and so could play against himself without even getting up from his chair.

For a long time the butler had been doing what he could to make the laird think of other things besides chess, and one evening he suggested that Hamilton should hold a summer party as they'd done in the days when her ladyship had been alive. This was one of the rare evenings when the laird, who generally preferred his own company, had offered the butler a glass of whisky, and now they were both seated beside the fish-pond, whisky glass in one hand and lit cigar in the other. The laird sat for some moments following one of the carp with his eyes before he turned to the butler and signalled his agreement that a summer party was an excellent idea, but that he should prefer a masquerade.

For an hour or two they sat there drawing up a guest list, but from the moment Hamilton mentioned that he wanted precisely 31 guests, the butler's suspicions were aroused, for he was all too aware that there were 32 pieces in a game of chess, and his two-hour ordeal on the chessboard at the laird's heartless behest was still fresh in his memory. The laird made no bones about the fact that one of the objects of the prospective masquerade was a chess tournament with live chessmen as a kind of after-dinner entertainment. An invitation was sent out several days later announcing that a chess masquerade was to be held at the Hamilton mansion at which the respective guest was requested to come dressed as a king, queen, castle, bishop, knight or pawn. The guests who were to be pawns really were sons of the local soil, eight farmers and eight farmers' wives, and the pieces were either army officers, senior officials or representatives of the nobility or aristocracy.

The butler wasn't surprised when everyone accepted the invitation, because although Lord Hamilton had been a grumbler of almost unrivalled proportions in recent years, both he and his house stood in high regard. With the single exception of the Duke of Argyll, who'd been invited to come dressed as a king, the laird outranked all his guests. For the farmers who'd been invited, the mere chance to visit the Hamilton estate was an occasion in itself, an almost inconceivable event in a society where, even beyond the confines of the chessboard, a very rigid system of rank and order held sway.

During the weeks prior to the party, which was to be held on Midsummer's Eve, the forthcoming masquerade was the sole topic of conversation in the locality. One of the farmers had to withdraw just a few days before the great event because of illness in the family, but there was no difficulty in finding another agricultural couple. There were plenty of farmers in the district, and they didn't have to be all that particular about their costumes – they were only going to play themselves, after all.

The great day came, and even during the banquet many new acquaintances were being cemented across social divides. After dinner, coffee and dessert were served in the garden, and shortly afterwards Lord Hamilton rang his loud bell and requested his guests' attention. Everyone was already aware that a game of chess was shortly to be played on the marble flags with themselves as the living chessmen, but the laird had first to allocate each one his or her particular place on the board.

At table, the seating had been fairly informal and at least seemingly unplanned, but this was far from how it was on the chessboard. First, the laird arranged the pawns: eight men and an equal number of women. Farmer MacLean was placed as a white pawn on a2 with his wife opposite as the black pawn on a7. On his right stood Mrs MacDonald on b2, and she faced her husband, the black pawn on b7. This carefully worked-out pattern meant that all spouses could observe one another across the chessboard, and they could also keep an eye on how their other half was doing with the farmer or farmer's wife to the left or right of them. Precisely the same logic was applied to the pieces. The white knight, Chief Constable MacLachlan, took up his position on b1 behind Mrs MacDonald and with his own wife as the black knight on b8 behind farmer MacDonald on b7. There were sixteen women and sixteen men on the board, there were two sides and two sexes facing each other, always divided by marriage. The only thing that disturbed this symmetry was the placing of the kings and queens. Lord Hamilton himself took up position as the white king on e1, he had the duchess on his left as the white queen on d1 and she was opposite the Duke of Argyll as the black king on e8. But Lady Hamilton was no longer amongst them. Hamilton had therefore given the role of black queen on d8 to a widow called MacQueen of whom he was rather fond and to whom, when by some rare chance he met her in town or at the cemetery, he sometimes chatted.

The two kings were the only people who ever decided which pieces to move, the other guests were no more than extras in the formal aspect of the game. Lord Hamilton had made no secret of the fact that the game itself might take some time, perhaps until well into the small hours, as both the duke and he were very experienced players, but the match was also to be a social game in which all the participants would have ample opportunity to get to know one another. Each chess piece was a living soul, and the guests were exhorted to entertain each other as best they could while they waited for the laird and the duke to make a move. Then gradually, as the chessmen fell, they could continue their informal socialising out in the spacious garden.

Lord Hamilton made his opening by ordering the white pawn – it was MacArthur – to advance two squares from e2 to e4, and the Duke of Argyll retaliated by moving Mrs MacArthur two squares up from e7 to e5, and the game had begun. The butler, chasing about the chessboard with drinks for those who wanted them, was the best witness to what ensued. He didn't find chess particularly engrossing himself, but soon – and with interest – he noted the rising suspense on the marble flags. Only one of the many climaxes will be highlighted here, but it was the most important one.

Mary Ann MacKenzie was an uncommonly beguiling young woman in her mid-twenties. She appeared on the chessboard as the white pawn on d2 opposite her husband Iain MacKenzie on d7. Iain was several years older than her and had always had a reputation as a bit of a Casanova. Even after marrying Mary Ann he'd had several mistresses, and he'd also flirted with several of the local married women, a couple of whom were present on the chessboard that night, a glass of sweet wine in their hands.

Over the years, everyone in the district had felt considerable sympathy for lovely Mary Ann. It was whispered that not only was MacKenzie unfaithful to her, but he was also a tyrant at home. So they were two diametrical opposites. Of Mary Ann it was said that she was probably the sweetest-natured young girl in the entire Scottish Highlands. She was so wonderfully captivating that it was no exaggeration to say that everyone who met her fell in love with her almost instantly. And not only men. There was something so singular about Mary Ann that even many women had to admit to having sleepless nights filled with tender thoughts of her.

If Iain was a potential cause for anxiety who'd at times threatened the stability of a number of local marriages, the same, paradoxically, could not be said of Mary Ann. When both a farmer and his wife felt themselves drawn to the selfsame person they usually remained on good terms, and so this mystifying woman often merely served to strengthen the marriage bond. It may perhaps be added that even the physical love between a couple could be spiced up by a common yearning for Mary Ann MacKenzie.

The very first to be taken on the board that evening at Lord Hamilton's was Mary Ann. And so she was free at once to wander round the large garden, to stroll in the exquisite labyrinth of clipped hedges or to stand by the pond and throw breadcrumbs to the fish. It was obvious that Iain felt uncomfortable about the freedom she'd been granted so early in the game. Right from the very start he followed his wife with a watchful gaze.

The next person who had to vacate the marble squares was Aileen MacBride, who'd been the black pawn on g7. Mary Ann was so intoxicated by the great garden, the lovely summer evening and all the wine she'd drunk, that she immediately took Mrs MacBride's hands and began to dance about the spacious lawn with her. Next, they ran hand in hand into the maze, and a number of the chess pieces caught glimpses of Aileen and Mary Ann standing there kissing and caressing one another. Hamish MacBride also took in what was happening behind the topiary but, far from feeling jealous, he rejoiced on his wife's behalf, for he felt certain that if he'd had the opportunity, he would have been the first to fondle Mary Ann himself. It was a long while before other guests were free to step off the marble slabs.

This is a very complex story and one that has been the subject of much commentary and analysis, but I'll give it here as briefly and concisely as humanly possible.

It was an enchanted evening, it was as if good spirits and guardian angels held their protective wings over what happened that Midsummer's Eve. The laird and the duke concentrated ever more deeply on their game as it moved slowly towards a conclusion, and gradually the garden became full of elated guests who'd been released from the chessboard. They all swarmed about Mary Ann, and even the officials and their wives who'd never met her before, now began to flock around her full of adulation and desire.

For the first time in her life Mary Ann felt free to be herself and give of her boundless love and, though there was no malice in her, she relished the sight of Iain continuing to be pushed this way and that on the marble squares by the duke. For Iain MacKenzie was kept on the chessboard right up to the moment, not long before dawn, when the Duke of Argyll checkmated Lord Hamilton. Mary Ann had good cause to fear that Iain would punish her when they got home, but she wasn't thinking that far ahead now. She thought instead of Iain's many years of unfaithfulness and decided that there was some justice in the world after all. It was still her night.

Gradually, as the pieces on the chessboard thinned, the party got more riotous and it was said that Mary Ann shared her love with everyone in the garden that night. All that time, Iain MacKenzie had to stand quietly on the marble slabs witnessing his own wife being belle of the ball and the object of an almost collective lust, a sensual sport in which, on this one night, Mary Ann was more than willing to be enveloped. In a sense, therefore, MacKenzie found himself standing in the corner. He was quite powerless to do anything, because it would have been thought deeply shameful to ask to be released from the chessboard before the game was over. It would have been like spurning Lord Hamilton's hospitality. But he raised his arm more and more often as a sign to the butler that he wanted the whisky glass in his hand replenished. Soon, though he wasn't as steady on his feet as before, he could still keep a constant watch on Mary Ann who, time and again, ran playfully in amongst the hedges of the maze with some new woman, man or married couple. Jealousy was banished from the laird's garden that night. Everyone loved Mary Ann and in a way, through her, everyone loved each other.

No sooner had Lord Hamilton conceded that the Duke of Argyll had checkmated him and shaken hands on the outcome, than Iain

MacKenzie lurched out into the garden to search for his wife. He discovered her sitting on the grass closely entwined with both the MacIvers, but he pulled her away and slapped her hard across the face with the flat of his hand. In a matter of seconds, however, he was surrounded by a dozen pawns and pieces from the chess game and Chief Constable MacLachlan, who'd served his time as the white knight, took him into custody.

Mary Ann didn't leave the Hamilton estate that morning. Her marriage to Iain was clearly irretrievable and the laird, who needed a new housekeeper anyway, offered her a home.

Hamilton recalled all the moves from his game with the Duke of Argyll, and for safety's sake he wrote them down, so that he could carefully study how he'd been beaten. He could often be seen in the garden reliving the game move by move on the marble slabs. On these occasions Mary Ann would sometimes sit on a chair by the fish-pond and talk to him.

For a while enthusiastic gossip circulated about Midsummer's Eve at Hamilton's house, and no one begrudged Mary Ann her final revenge for Iain's many years of depravity. But if good spirits and guardian angels had watched over Hamilton's garden that night, ogres and demons took a hand in its sequel. Not long after, there was a series of dreadful murders in the district and after the third, Chief Constable MacLachlan noted that all of the victims had occupied a place on Hamilton's marble slabs some weeks earlier. Hamilton's butler got in touch with the chief constable after the fifth murder to tell him that the deceased had also all been killed in precisely the same order as the laird's guests had been knocked off the chessboard. These were two pawns, two bishops and a knight. There was only one exception to this sequence: the very first who'd run out into the garden that Midsummer's Eve — Mary Ann MacKenzie. MacLachlan, who'd never forgotten the ethereal Mary Ann, noted the fact with interest. He had no difficulty guessing why this brutal serial killer had spared the charming young woman.

Quite the reverse, he thought, it wasn't difficult to hazard that the motive for all the murders was that the murderer – or murderers – wished to eliminate all possible competition and have the beautiful goddess completely to themselves. This, in turn, meant that there were a great many suspects to be considered.

The sixth and seventh murders were committed, continuing the macabre replay of the fatal chess game. The police now knew at any given time who would be the next victim, and gave the threatened individual a certain degree of protection, but they were still unable to prevent the murders from taking place.

The victims were nearly always done to death outdoors in forest or farmland, and always with a sharp butcher's knife. Soon, almost half the guests from Hamilton's fancy dress ball had been killed, and the serial killer began to get closer to the laird and the duke, not to mention the chief constable. He knew very well that he'd been the sixteenth piece to be taken on the board.

Naturally enough, one of the first suspects was Iain MacKenzie who'd been so irrevocably humiliated by his wife that fateful night, and had now lost her for good. Apart from the laird and the duke, MacKenzie was the last piece left standing on the chessboard and, in theory at least, he might have been able to remember every move in the game. But when the thirteenth and fourteenth murders took place while MacKenzie was in police custody, he was set free with a pat on the shoulder.

The laird himself was questioned by the police. It was he who had lost the game, not without a little disgruntlement, and he was also one of the few who knew the game move by move. The police also wanted to ask the laird why he had organised such a bizarre masquerade in the first place.

When the butler was brought in for questioning at the police station, they raked over certain inconsistencies between his own statements and the laird's, but he was never on the list of suspects. He was, however, able to tell the police that, both before and after that calamitous Midsummer's Eve, he'd been concerned about Hamilton's mental health.

The farmer and his wife who'd cried off only a few days before the party were also brought in and eliminated from the enquiry.

She was finally caught red-handed after gaining entry to MacIver's barn and stabbing the farmer in the chest with a butcher's knife.

It had been easy enough for Mary Ann to gain entry to the local farms, lawyers' offices and large estates. Nor had she found any difficulty in enticing the women and men of the place out into forests and moors.

Chief Constable MacLachlan was an experienced police officer, but even he had to ask Mary Ann what her motive for the most brutal series of killings in Scotland's history could have been.

The bewitchingly beautiful Mary Ann told him it was shame.

It had been an enchanted evening, and she clearly recalled all the lips she'd kissed and all the passionate embraces she, with tenderness and desire, had allowed herself to be swept up in, but subsequently she had felt ashamed of her immorality. She could have elected to take her own life, but that wouldn't have made things any better. Mary Ann couldn't bear the thought that any of the laird's guests should go on living with the recollection of her chasing about the hedges of Hamilton's garden giving herself to half of Scotland.

Many attended and wept bitterly when Mary Ann was hanged at Glasgow a few months later.

That September I began to study history. Sometimes I invited a girl student home for cheese and wine or omelettes and lager. I could grill steaks as well, and I could make stew, fish soup and pickled herring.

I was just waiting for Maria to come and tell me that she'd got the job she'd applied for in Stockholm. Then she rang one evening and asked if she could come round. When she turned up, she was carrying a large bunch of yellow roses. They were for me. It seemed strange. I didn't know what she wanted, but I knew that something was up.

We sat leaning across the kitchen table holding hands. I'd switched off all the lights. Only a single lighted candle stood on the table between us. We'd drunk a bottle of cheap red wine.

I was glad to have Maria back, but I wanted her to get to the point. First, she told me she'd got the job in Stockholm and that she'd be moving in December. I thought that I could learn to live in Sweden too, but before I was able to speak Maria said something that shut the idea of Stockholm out for ever.

She looked into my eyes and said that she had a favour to ask of me. It was something that would last our entire lifetime, she said.

I felt a tremor pass through my body. For the first time I'd been able to embrace the notion of something that might last my whole life. I liked the sound of the word 'last', it was a beautiful word.

'I want to take a child to Stockholm with me,' she said.

Once more I felt that Maria was the only woman I'd ever met whom I didn't always understand. It was what I liked so much about her. It's impossible to love anyone you always understand completely.

'I want you to give me a child, Petter,' she said.

I didn't grasp the significance of what she was saying. I was still thinking about what it would be like to move to Stockholm. Should I sell the Oslo flat? Or simply let it out?

But then Maria said that she didn't want to spend her entire life with one man. She was just like me, she said. Maria knew me intimately, I'd told her about all my female visitors. I felt I was seeing myself in a mirror.

Maria wanted to have a child by me. She said I was the

only man she could contemplate as a father to her child, she'd known that since we first met at Ullevålseter, but she couldn't tie herself to me. She asked me to make her pregnant. She asked me to inseminate her.

I laughed. I thought it was a rather neat idea, and one so absolutely in my spirit. Procreation without commitment was right up my street.

We sat there a long time talking the matter over, but not at all in an earnest way. We were laughing and joking. Maria wanted us to sleep together again, and the idea was alluring. We could sleep together until Maria got pregnant. Then she'd have to leave for Stockholm.

Despite all this, I wasn't ready to father a child. I wonder if I ever have been. The mere thought of looking into my own child's eyes struck me as awful. I hadn't liked having my head patted and I hadn't enjoyed having my cheek pinched. So how would I manage being the one doing the patting?

I mulled over these aspects as well. I didn't want a child, but I could help Maria. The more we talked, the more convinced I became that her idea was a brilliant one. She stipulated that we had to make a pact. She said we had to promise not to try to find one another after she'd moved to Stockholm. We would never be able to meet again. I wasn't even to have her address. And, most importantly, we were to swear that even the child's paternity was to be a secret between the two of us. All I was to be told was whether it was a boy or a girl.

I was so fascinated by this scheme that I felt the blood begin to pound in my veins. Maria was not just my equal, I felt she excelled me in talent and audacity.

Giving a woman a child that wasn't to be mine suited me perfectly. I'd always liked spreading myself, emptying myself, but I'd never been much interested in what I might call copyright. I'd never had any need to be applauded for what I did or initiated, not even when I was little. I received no ovation for the taxis I ordered. Ordering taxis had been a wonderful idea, but no one had thanked me for it afterwards.

Now we'd be able to meet often in the days to come. That alone was a great inducement. I've never found it easy to look more than a few days into the future. I've looked backwards and to the sides, but I've never taken much account of the days to come. I told Maria that I accepted her conditions. It would be an honour to make her pregnant, I said. It would give me such enormous pleasure. We had a long laugh at that. We guffawed. We got randier and randier.

Several glorious weeks followed, and even now they feel like the only weeks of my life when I've been truly alive.

We termed our special relationship an *ad hoc* romance. We couldn't stay in bed making children all day, but we spent the entire twenty-four hours together. We went for long walks in the city and in the forest, and I narrated some of my zaniest stories. Maria had a particular penchant for an involved tale about a jeweller who committed a posthumous and thoroughly premeditated triple murder. I actually told the story I'd sold to the author in Club 7, too. After all, Maria was leaving the country.

I had to tell some of the stories twice or three times. Maria said she wanted to try to learn them by heart. The only problem was that I was never able to tell a story exactly the same way twice. At times like these Maria would leap in and prompt me. She couldn't understand how she could be better at remembering what I'd said and the exact way I'd expressed it. I explained that the only real skill I possessed was improvisation.

Soon came the day we'd both been waiting for, Maria with joy and I with sorrow. Her pregnancy test was positive and Maria opened her arms wide and rejoiced. Jokingly she said that I'd be a 'marvellous daddy'. We cackled loudly at that as well.

Maria remained in Oslo a couple of months more before moving to Stockholm. We saw less of each other again. She sometimes phoned and asked me over to the campus to tell her a story, and I never made excuses, but it was odd to think that a part of me had already taken root in her body.

Then Maria went. She rang before she left. I didn't go with her to the station.

★

I was the right man to give a woman a child he wasn't to share. Why shouldn't I let Maria have the child she wanted? It was easy. It was free. It cost me nothing. I reckoned it was I who should be grateful. But everything has two sides. I never imagined I'd have to pay so dearly for it. I wasn't allowed to see Maria again.

However, it took several years before our solemn pact came into full force. She came to Oslo with her daughter four times in all. Maria simply called her 'Poppet', but she'd obviously given her another name as well. I imagined that Maria used a pet name just to keep her real one from me. At our final meeting, the child was almost three. That was when the pact was renewed and it had to be the very last time I saw her. Maria's idea was that the little girl mustn't form any impression of her father. And for that matter I wasn't to form any real image of her either, as I wasn't a proper father.

She was a sweet little girl. I didn't think she took after Maria or me, but I could see a clear resemblance to my mother; she had the same high cheekbones and the same widely spaced eyes. I felt my mother was reborn, and that it was I who'd given her a new chance. I realised, of course, that I was fantasising.

The last time I met Maria and the little girl was on a warm June evening in 1975. We only had a few hours together, and we spent them by Lake Sognsvann. We'd brought along prawns, French bread and white wine. Maria and I sat chatting about the old days while the little girl splashed about at the water's edge with an inflatable swan. When she ran up from the water for her juice and biscuits, both mother and daughter permitted me to wrap her in a bath towel and dry her. I helped her with her dress too, it was the least I could do. Maria had once said that I'd make a 'marvellous daddy'.

Poppet sat down on the towel between us, and I began to tell her a long fairy tale, or a *saga* as I called it. She was laughing even before I really got going. I don't know if she understood what I said, and perhaps that was why she was laughing, but I tried to use some Swedish words to make things easier for her.

I told of a small girl about her own age, who was called Panina Manina and whose father was the ringmaster of the finest circus in the whole, wide world. The circus came from a faraway land, but once upon a time, long ago, it was on its way to Stockholm where, by invitation of the King and Queen of Sweden, it was to set up its big top in a park right in the middle of the Swedish capital. All the circus trailers drove up through Sweden in one long line, and in the procession were elephants and sea-lions, bears and giraffes, horses and camels, dogs and monkeys. The trailers also contained clowns and jugglers, fakirs and tight-rope walkers, animal tamers and bare-back riders, magicians and musicians. The only child in this whole great caravan was Panina Manina. She was treated like a little princess because she was the ringmaster's daughter, and it was said that destiny had decreed that she would become a famous circus artiste.

The little girl sat bolt upright listening to my story, but she never said anything, so I couldn't be certain how much she was taking in. I assumed that at least she was getting something of the atmosphere of the fairy tale. I glanced at Maria, and she indicated that it was all right for me to continue. I think she was pleased that the little girl, too, could share at least one story. Even Metre Man had settled himself against a tree so that he could hear the rest of the tale. As he sat down, he raised his green hat and gave me a confidential wink. I think he was in a good mood. Perhaps it was the first time he'd felt like one of the family.

I told how all the big circus lorries and trailers halted for dinner by a large lake deep in the Swedish forests and, while they were there, the ringmaster's daughter wanted to paddle in the water. The ringmaster thought that one of the clowns was keeping a watchful eye on her, but the clown had misunderstood and thought the animal tamer was supposed to be looking after Panina Manina while the adults roasted wild boar steaks on a huge camp fire. At all events, when the great convoy was due to continue its journey to Stockholm a few hours later, nobody could find her. They searched for her all evening and night, and many of the animals were let loose to see if they could pick up her scent, but all to no avail. After searching high and low for Panina Manina most of the next day, everyone came to the conclusion she must have drowned in the lake. For hours, two camels stood at the water's edge drinking, they drank and drank, and there was a general belief that this was because they recognised the smell of Panina Manina in the water, and they were probably trying to drink the lake dry. But at last the camels' thirst was slaked and the ringmaster's daughter was still missing, and remained so. It was said that the ringmaster cried himself to sleep for many a sad year afterwards, because Panina Manina had been the apple of his eye, he had been fonder of her than all the rest of the circus put together.

I pretended to wipe away a tear, and I think the little girl gazed up at me. It seemed she had at least understood the last thing I'd said; after all, she'd been paddling down there at the water's edge herself quite recently, so I hurriedly went on:

But Panina Manina hadn't drowned. She'd simply gone off to do a little exploring while the grown-ups sat in front of the fire drinking wine and eating wild boar meat. She followed a nice little path into the forest, and soon her legs were so tired that she sat down in the ling between the tall trees. As she sat there listening to the doves cooing and the owls hooting, she fell into a deep sleep. When she awoke, she imagined she'd only dropped off for a few minutes, but in reality she'd slept all through the night and more besides, for the sun was now high in the sky. Panina Manina took the path again to find her way back to the camp fire, but she wasn't able to find a single circus trailer, and soon she was lost in the forest. Late that evening she arrived at a small homestead with a little red house and a flagpole flying the Swedish flag. A pink caravan stood parked in front of the red wooden building, and perhaps it was this that attracted Panina Manina's attention, for to her it looked rather like a circus trailer. Although she was only three, she went up to the caravan and knocked at the door. When no one answered, she crawled up a small flight of stone steps leading up to the red house and knocked on the door there. It opened and out came an old woman. Panina Manina wasn't frightened; maybe this was because she was a real circus girl.

She looked up at the strange lady and said that she'd got separated from her daddy – but she spoke in a language the woman couldn't understand, because Panina Manina came from a faraway land that the old lady had never visited. Panina Manina hadn't eaten for almost two days, and now she put her little hands to her mouth to show that she was hungry. At that the woman realised that she was lost in the forest and let the little girl in. She gave her herring and meatballs, bread and blackberry juice. Panina Manina was so hungry and thirsty that she ate and drank like a grown-up. When night came, the woman made up a bed for her and, because they couldn't talk to each other properly, she sat down by the bed and sang her a lullaby until she fell into a deep sleep. As she had no idea what the girl's name was she simply called her 'Poppy'.

Poppet glanced up at me again. Perhaps it was because I was miming the way Panina Manina ate herring and meatballs, but it might also have been because she had noticed that the girl in the story had been called 'Poppy'. I wasn't certain she'd understood much of the story itself, but I went on:

Panina Manina lived in the little house for many years. No one in the whole of Sweden managed to find out who her mother and father were and, as the years passed, Panina Manina's memory of the ringmaster grew dimmer and dimmer. Soon she was talking fluent Swedish and had forgotten her own language because she hadn't got anyone to speak it to now. But – and now I raised a forefinger to show that there was something important I'd left out – the woman in the house had an old crystal ball hidden away in a cupboard in the bedroom. Once, many years before, she'd made her living as a fortune-teller in a large amusement park at Lund. Now she got out the crystal ball and foretold that one day Poppy would become a famous tight-rope walker.

So, she began to train her to balance on everything from planks and ropes to buckets and tubs, and one day she was ready to show her skills to a real ringmaster. This was thirteen years after Poppy had first knocked on her door. The old woman had read in the newspaper that a famous foreign circus had arrived in Stockholm, and one day the pair of them travelled to the city to try their luck. It was the same circus from far away that had come to Stockholm thirteen years earlier, but Panina Manina no longer had the faintest recollection of ever being part of a circus. The foreign ringmaster was impressed by the Swedish girl's abilities and so she became part of the circus. Neither Panina Manina nor the ringmaster had any idea she was really his daughter.

Maria was giving me a quizzical look. She had always been especially interested in how I ended my stories. Perhaps she was particularly concerned this time as there was a pair of small ears between us.

Now, I went on, blood is thicker than water, as the saying goes, and maybe that was why the ringmaster and Panina Manina hit it off right from the start. At all events, Panina Manina made up her mind to travel back with the circus to the faraway land, where she soon became a famous tight-rope dancer. One evening when she was performing on her tight-rope high above the ring, she threw a quick glance down at the ringmaster who was standing in front of the big circus orchestra with a whip in his hands, and there and then she realised that the ringmaster was really her father, so she hadn't quite forgotten him after all. Such insights are often called 'moments of truth', I explained. In her confusion, Panina Manina lost her balance and fell, smack-bang-wallop, right down into the ring. When the ringmaster came rushing up to see if she'd hurt herself, she stretched up her arms to him and with a loud, heart-rending wail cried out: 'Daddy! Daddy!'

Poppet peered up at me in astonishment and laughed, but I didn't think she'd understood much of what I'd been saying. Not so Maria. She glared at me furiously. It was obvious she hadn't liked the final line of the fairy tale.

The sun was about to set on our little family reunion. We packed up our things and walked to the tram. For a time the little girl skipped along the path in front of us. 'Daddy, daddy!' she muttered. Then Maria took my hand and squeezed it. I noticed her eyes were full of tears. When we got down into the city again, we went our separate ways. That was the last time I saw Maria and the child. I've never heard from them since.

Writers' Aid

Twenty-six years later, I sit before a large double window looking down at the coast and out across the ocean. The sun is low in the sky, and a gossamer of gold leaf has settled over the bay. A boat carrying a handful of tourists is heading for the breakwater. They've been to inspect the emerald-green cave a few miles down the coast.

As for me, I've been for a long stroll through the many lemon groves and on up the Valley of the Mills high above the town. The people here are friendly and kind. A woman dressed in black leant out of a window and offered me a glass of lemon liqueur.

I'm on my guard. Up in the valley I didn't meet a soul, but whether because of that or despite it, I still didn't feel safe. Several times I stopped and looked behind me. If anyone has followed me from Bologna, this narrow valley bottom with all its old, derelict paper-mills would be the perfect place to finish me off.

For safety's sake I keep the door of my room locked. If anyone got in they could easily push me out of a window. The sills are low, it's a long way down to the old coast road and the traffic is heavy. It might look like suicide or an accident.

There aren't many guests here. Besides me, only three couples and a German of about my own age went down to dinner. Presumably it will get busier in a few days' time, over the Easter weekend.

The German sent me expectant glances. Perhaps he

wished to make contact as we were the only two on our own. I wondered if I'd seen him before. I speak fluent German.

Before I went to bed later that evening, I took care to lock my door. I avoided the bar. I have my own supply of alcohol in my room. There's already one empty bottle in the corner. Should I feel lonely, I've always got Metre Man to talk to. He has a tendency to pop up as soon as I feel in need of company. I've been here four nights.

The Spider has been caught in his own web. First he spins a trap of finely woven silk. Then he loses his footing and gets stuck to his own web.

★

It strikes me now, as I write, that Maria betrayed me utterly. In a way she excelled me in cynicism. She must have known that I'd never be able to love another woman and she also made sure there was no going back. She'd placed something between us.

It's the first time I've thought of Maria in this way. It surprises me. As if only now I've begun to pull myself together after my mother's death. Father died a year ago. I believe I was very fond of my mother.

I continue to live with the feeling that there is something important I've forgotten. It's as if all my life I've tried hard not to remember something that happened when I was very young. But it's still not completely buried, it goes on swimming about in the murky depths beneath the thin ice I've been dancing on. I no sooner relax and try to get hold of the thing I'm trying to forget, than a good idea materialises and I begin spinning a new story.

My own consciousness causes me anxiety more and more often. It's like a phantom I can't control.

It was all that imagination of mine that frightened Maria, too. She was fascinated, but frightened.

★

When Maria had left, the world was my oyster, there was a feeling of freedom about it. It was a long time before I re-established my contacts with girls and I'd given up my studies because I felt far too adult to be a student. Never, since my mother died, had the world seemed so wide open.

I often thought about the young writer who'd stood me a bottle of wine and paid a hundred kroner for the book synopsis. I had dozens of similar pieces at home. His novel was published a couple of years later and got good reviews.

I hung about a bit in Club 7, or in the arty Casino bar, or the Tostrupkjelleren which was the journalists' watering hole, as well as that huge painters' studio-cum-restaurant, Kunstnernes Hus. It was easy to get talking to people. Soon I knew everyone in town who was worth talking to. The problem was that at that early stage I was perennially short of money.

I was considered a bright young spark teeming with ideas, and that was no more than the truth. The people I talked to were always older than me. Many of them were dreamers and idlers, and most had artistic ambitions, or at least artistic pretensions. To me they seemed narrow-minded. A few had published an anthology of poems or a novel, others said they 'wrote' or that they 'wanted to write'. If they didn't say this they felt they lacked legitimacy. These were the people amongst whom I conducted my earliest trans-actions.

When anyone I was drinking with said that they 'wrote' or 'wanted to write', I would sometimes ask what they wanted to write about. In most cases they couldn't say. I found this puzzling. Even then – and increasingly since – I found something comic about the way society spawns people who are both able and willing writers, but who have nothing to offer. Why do people want to 'write' when they openly and honestly admit that they have nothing to impart? Couldn't they do something else? What is this desire to do things without being active? In my case the situation has always been the reverse. I've always been gravid, but have never had any wish to produce offspring. The last is meant literally, too. The episode with Maria was about something quite different. She was the one I needed.

I kept a diary at the time. But it was not for public consumption, merely a few jottings I made for my own benefit, a kind of musing. In it I wrote:

I shall never write a novel. I wouldn't be able to concentrate on one story. If I began to spin a fable, it would immediately suck in four or eight others. Then there would be a veritable cacophony to hold in check, with dense layers of frame stories and a myriad of interpolated histories with several narrators on different narrative levels, or what some people call Chinese Boxes. Because I'm unable to stop thinking, I can't prevent myself from spawning ideas. It's something almost organic, something that comes and goes of its own accord. I'm drowning in my own fecundity, I'm constantly at bursting point. New notions bleed unendingly from my brain. Perhaps that's why I've taken a liking to bar stools. There I can relieve myself.

And so a symbiosis grew up. I found it easy to hatch out new ideas and associations. It was much harder not to. But it wasn't like this for the people who wanted to 'write'. Many of them could go for months or years without finding a single original idea to write about. I was surrounded by people who had an enormous desire to express themselves, but the desire was greater than the expression, the need bigger than the message. I saw an almost limitless market for my services. But how was the business to be organised?

On the very day Maria left for Stockholm, I went into town with some of my work. It was a collection of twenty aphorisms. I wanted to test the market, and I wanted to try out my own sales pitch. My idea was to trade the aphorisms one by one: a beer for each, for example. I have to admit the aphorisms were good, very good indeed. So I was willing to swap an exceptionally elegant aphorism for half a litre of beer – and thereafter evermore to forget that I had penned it. It was largely a question of finding the right person, and that was dependent on my ability to strike up a discreet conversation. Now I had a pressing motive: I'd used up my last few kroner on Maria and had no money to go out drinking.

Late that afternoon I bumped into an author in front of the National Theatre, whom for these purposes I shall call Johannes, and who was some fifteen years older than me. We'd spoken on many previous occasions and I knew he regarded me as a genius. I think he'd already realised that his writing could benefit from a chat with me. He'd once asked me when I intended to make my début. He asked this in a voice that would have been better suited to an enquiry about my sexual début. 'Never,' I'd replied. I told him I'd never make my literary début. This made a deep impression on him. Few people said such things in those days.

I asked Johannes if I could buy him a drink. I didn't mention that I had no money. If it all went wrong, I would have to leave the discovery for when the bill arrived. No one had ever caught me in a lie. But I was pretty confident things would work out. Although it hadn't been my intention, I made up my mind to offer him the entire collection of aphorisms because the notion that Maria was gone had again washed over me and I couldn't chance not having enough to drink that evening. From Johannes' point of view the aphorisms could prove to be worth a fortune. If he used them properly and eked them out with material of his own, they'd give him a new identity. He had published two novels in six years and neither was particularly good. In the early seventies it was rare for a novel to contain twenty aphorisms.

We went down to the Casino. Luckily it wasn't very full, but those present were actors or authors – topped up with regulars who aspired to be actors or authors. We found a quiet corner.

After a while I repeated one of the aphorisms from memory. 'Who wrote that?' Johannes asked. I pointed to myself. Then I gave him another one. 'Fabulous,' he said. I reeled off yet another. 'But I thought you said you didn't write?' he queried. I shook my head. I told him I'd said that I'd never make my début. I explained that I didn't want to be an author. Now it was his turn to shake his head. Within those four walls the statement 'I don't want to be an author' had probably never been uttered before.

Every clique and sub-culture has its own set of self-evident assumptions. The circle Johannes moved in didn't contain anyone who said he didn't want to be an author; eventually, and only after many years, one might conceivably acknowledge it as something one couldn't achieve. It's not the same everywhere. There are still rural enclaves in odd backwaters of the world in which the opposite assertion would sound just as demented. Doubtless there are still some farmers who would be incensed if the heir apparent came in from the outlying fields or the hay-making one day and announced that he wanted to be a writer.

Nowadays most secondary school pupils say they want to

be famous, and they mean it too. Just twenty years ago such a statement would have been seen as quite brazen. Cultural norms can be turned upside down within a single generation. In the fifties and sixties you couldn't go round with impunity saying you wanted to be famous when you grew up. You were grateful to become a doctor or a policeman. If you did aspire to fame, you'd have to explain exactly what you wanted to be famous for: the contribution had to precede the fame. This doesn't happen now. First you decide to be famous, then as an afterthought, how you'll achieve it. Whether you deserve the fame or not is a virtual irrelevancy. At worst, you make your way as a bastard on a TV docusoap, or, descending into the ultimate slime, break the law in some sensational way. But I've pre-empted this development; it's as if I've known that one day being famous would become vulgar. I've always eschewed vulgarity.

'You're quite a character, Petter,' Johannes said.

I placed the twenty aphorisms before him, and Johannes drank them in. He exuded envy.

'You wrote these yourself?' he asked. 'You didn't get them from someone else?'

I shrugged demonstratively. The very idea of taking stuff that others had written and passing it off as my own was such an anathema that I found it hard to hide my disgust. I didn't even lay claim to the things I *had* written.

I'd got him interested, that was obvious, but I still had some complex manoeuvring to do. I had decided to do the deal properly and there is always something special about the first time. I was aware that I was in the process of establishing a permanent business. I was being put to the test – this was to be my living. If I failed now, it would be more difficult next time.

I told him that, under certain conditions, he could have

the twenty aphorisms to use as his own. He gawped: 'Are you mad, Petter?'

I gave him a quick lecture. I made him understand once and for all that I was serious about not becoming a writer. He grasped that I was the victim of some rare kind of bashfulness. I told him I couldn't bear the thought of living in the public gaze, that I felt happier in the wings, that I would never exchange my anonymity for money. I went on to predicate this on a more contemporary political ideal as well. 'I've come to the conclusion that it isn't right to stand out,' I said. 'Why should an articulate élite raise their heads above the masses? Isn't it better for everyone to have a collective working spirit?' I spoke of the rank and file and of the grass roots, and maybe I used the term 'on the shop floor', which was then a very resonant expression, a really forceful idiom. I also mentioned medieval artistic anonymity. 'Nobody knows who wrote some of the old Norse myths,' I said. 'And in the end, Johannes, does it really matter?'

He shook his head. Johannes was a Marxist-Leninist. Then I quickly added that the path I'd chosen for myself was strictly a personal position. I said I'd read both his novels and that obviously I could see the value of someone becoming the mouthpiece of the people, only that it wasn't me.

It had begun to dawn on Johannes that he might soon be standing out in the street in possession of those twenty aphorisms. But there was still a lot to arrange, and I tackled the pecuniary side first. I told him I was hard up and that I was willing to sell the aphorisms for fifty kroner apiece, but that he could buy all twenty for eight hundred. At first I thought I'd pitched it too high. Eight hundred kroner was a lot of money in those days, both for students and authors. But Johannes didn't look as if he was going to back out.

After all, they were twenty uncommonly pithy aphorisms – I'd spent a whole morning working them up. I said that naturally he was free to choose the ones he liked best and pay for them individually, but on the other hand it really did seem a shame to split them up. I'd had Johannes specially in mind and didn't like the thought of relinquishing my copyright in things I'd written to more than one person.

'Super,' said Johannes. 'I'll buy the lot.'

Then I said something about feeling a little sullied by our financial arrangement, but reminded him that we were still living in a capitalist society and that a piece of intellectual property was indeed regarded as a commodity. 'This is not very different from an artist taking payment for his paintings,' I said. 'They change ownership too, and the artist can't have any claim to the paintings he's already sold.' I believe Johannes was glad to be reminded of the normality of our arrangements.

He said: 'I can't preclude the possibility that I'll use some of these in a novel I'm writing at the moment . . .'

'Perfectly all right,' I replied. 'You'll make money out of them, a lot maybe, and good luck to you. It's not unusual to sell a painting for much more than one originally paid for it. It's what's known as a good investment.'

Fortunately he was the one who brought up the most sensitive matter. He pointed at the sheaf of papers in front of him and said: 'But how can I be sure you won't let the cat out of the bag by saying that these aphorisms are really your work?'

I said I was only too pleased that the aphorisms would get published and reminded him that I wanted to stay out of the limelight. I also mentioned that I had several other things at home, jottings of various kinds, and that it wasn't inconceivable that we'd return to these on a subsequent occasion.

If I didn't keep quiet about the aphorisms he took with him today, I'd ruin the opportunity to sell him something in the future.

This last point was an important one. I had to emphasise that I had no intention of selling anything I'd written to anyone other than Johannes. This was vital for building up a sales network of many clients. Each one had to feel that he or she was unique, my sole and only favourite.

I had reason to believe that this strategy would work for many years to come. Authors don't go round announcing that they employ a ghost-writer. They want to seem like original and thoroughly authentic individuals.

Correctly handled, there was no reason to fear that my customers would begin to shoot their mouths off to one another. I needn't be afraid of the web unravelling, the threads would only be spun between me and each of my clients. There would be none to connect my customers with one another.

Johannes looked about furtively, then he leant across the table and whispered: 'Two hundred cash, and I'll give you a cheque for six hundred. OK?'

I nodded. I was particularly grateful for some cash and not solely because of the beer I had to pay for. Though the evening was still young, I recalled that the bank was closed. With discreet movements, almost as if he was performing a ballet, he took out the two hundred kroner in notes and his cheque book. He wrote out the cheque as slowly and thoughtfully as if he was signing a tax return, then pushed the cheque and notes across the table towards me, and I folded the sheets and pushed them over the table to Johannes. Again he squinted round the room, but he didn't see the little man with the bamboo cane who was about to run under a waiter's feet.

Johannes quickly stowed the folded pages in the inner

pocket of his jacket. 'Shall we go?' he asked. But I said I was going to have another beer. 'Thank you very much, Petter,' were his parting words. With that he got up and began walking towards the exit. As he turned the corner towards the cloakroom I saw him pat his breast, presumably to make sure he really did have the gilt-edged sheaf of papers in his pocket. I thought I might photocopy his cheque before I cashed it. I didn't quite know why, but I had the feeling it might be useful to keep some souvenirs.

It was a good piece of business for Johannes. His return on those aphorisms was many many times his outlay. But that's the way it is with any sort of paper investment, you never know what it may be worth in the future. But I needed the money right there and then. Maria was on the train to Stockholm.

Johannes died a short time ago. He will be remembered for his precise, almost lapidary axioms.

I had already decided not to feed any single author with more than one genre. It would have seemed highly implausible if the city had suddenly turned into a literary cornucopia. There was only one stud, but his rut was enough to inseminate an entire flock of writers.

And so, with one exception, I fed Johannes solely with a variety of adages, thoughts and aphorisms, or with 'spice' as he once called it. Since he was one of the moving spirits behind the Marxist-Leninists' May Day procession, I also gave him several clever slogan and catchword ideas over the years, though I never took any payment for them.

The exception was a plot for a story set in Vietnam. The sheet of notes he got for a hundred kroner ran something like this:

Two identical twins are born a few minutes apart in a small village

*in the Mekong Delta at the beginning of the 1950s. After their
mother's rape and murder at the hands of a French soldier before the
boys are six months old, they are adopted by separate families and
grow up without seeing each other. One twin joins the FNL, and
the other the American-backed government force. After the Tet
offensive the twins come face to face in the jungle. Both are on
reconnaissance prior to a major action but as yet it's only the two
brothers who've clashed. They are identical in appearance, and each
recognises his twin brother. Now, one of them has to die. But the
two soldiers are equally good with their knives, they have precisely
the same genetic characteristics, and manage to wound each other
fatally.*

*Some useful ideas: dwell on the choice facing the two of them, the
logic of war. The man who doesn't kill his brother risks getting
killed himself. Do the brothers manage to say anything to each other
before their last gasp? Do they gain any new insight? (A short
dialogue here?) Don't forget the battle scene: the two dying twins
who once were at peace with one another in their mother's womb
and later, when they each suckled at one of her breasts, but who
have now killed each other. The circle is complete. They were born
in the same hour and now their blood mingles in a single pool. Who
finds the twins? What reaction does the discovery provoke?*

Johannes used the story, but turned it into a novella. When
I read it in a literary periodical a year later, I thought it was
well written, and I was particularly impressed with his
detailed knowledge of military hardware and all the telling
background descriptions of Vietnam. But it made me rather
depressed all the same.

Johannes' version of the story ended, of course, with the
twin who represented the army of liberation being unable to
kill his twin brother, even though this brother had enlisted
as a lackey of US imperialism. And so he'd been brutally
liquidated himself.

Throughout the novella the words 'sly' and 'heroic' were used repeatedly, but never of the same twin. Johannes had known how to deploy the fact that the twins were identical. He had used the story to demonstrate how little effect inherited characteristics have on a person's development.

I can't say I was shocked by this turn of events, for it was hardly surprising. That was the way a lot of literature was written in the seventies. Literature's job wasn't principally to debate problems. It was supposed to be uplifting.

★

During the next few years I established myself on a national basis and I also made a few contacts in the other Scandinavian countries as well. It took longer to go international, that was the next step.

One important principle was that I couldn't sell the same notes more than once. That would have been spotted. What a spectacle it would have been if two detective novels by two separate authors based on exactly the same plot had appeared in the same year! The thought struck me occasionally and it was a seductive one, because it would indubitably have been interesting to see, just once, what two authors made of the same idea.

I also had to be careful which stories I told in company. I couldn't run the risk of a critic pointing out that a recently published novel was based on a story which had been doing the rounds for ages and which the reviewer had most recently heard related across a table at the Tostrupkjelleren. This forced me to segregate the stories I could tell myself from the plots that were earmarked for sale. I had to curb my oral development. Living with this limitation was an excellent challenge. It pushed me ever harder to invent something new the whole time.

Right from the start I had to live with one big exception to this rule. I'd told so many good stories to Maria that I didn't feel I could keep them all back. If Maria read Norwegian novels during the eighties and nineties, she'd have chuckled quite regularly. In more recent years she'd also have been able to reminisce about the days when she nestled in my arms, by reading various foreign novels. I have several film synopses on my conscience too, or on my list of credits, depending on how you look at it. I like the thought of Maria going to the cinema and watching an epic cinematic version of one of the many stories I made up for her after we'd made love. I need no other copyright acknowledgement.

So from the first, Maria was the only one able to pinpoint me as The Spider. I never told my authors about Maria, and I never told Maria about them, even though my business was well established by the time we last met. But I felt I was safe with her – she had used my services too. Maria's darling child was conceived by the Holy Spirit. That was her little secret that she didn't want revealed. Perhaps she was as scared of it becoming common knowledge as Johannes was of the whole city finding out I'd written the twenty aphorisms that had added zest to the novel that proved to be his literary breakthrough. In this regard but only in this, Maria was in exactly the same boat as Johannes.

When a thing was sold, it was gone. This didn't pose a problem. The idea that I'd ever run out of ideas never occurred to me, it was the only thing I simply couldn't conceive. I'd been much alone in childhood, I'd had my own flat since I was eighteen, I'd been in training ever since I went to nursery school.

However, I made a point of keeping a photocopy of all the notes I sold. They were kept in separate ring-binders marked 'SOLD'. On the top of each page I wrote who I'd sold them to and how much for. In the early days this was the only system of receipts I used, but that was before I realised that it was possible one day for a counter-force to build up, to equalise the pressure that arose from within me. It was before I began to carry a dictaphone in my inside pocket when I talked to authors, and before I began to tape telephone conversations. However, I did keep photocopies of every cheque I'd received right back to my earliest transactions. And I might as well make it clear that those, too, are kept in my bank box, together with the tapes.

The enterprise got going just at the time when photocopiers were coming on to the market. For a short while I was dependent on the coin-operated machines at the university or in the library, but it wasn't long before I had my own Rank Xerox. When personal computers made their appearance in the 1980s, the office work became much simpler, and when I went international in earnest, I never travelled anywhere without a powerful laptop.

I had to accept being the centre of a large circle of acquaintance. This was a bit of a trial sometimes, but it wasn't onerous. I was a sociable person, I was well liked, and I rarely found I had to pay my share of restaurant bills. I couldn't always explain why myself but, whenever a bill was presented, someone had almost always settled up for me. That was just the way it was.

I had a reputation as a fount of ideas. If they'd only known! None of them could see more than the tip of the iceberg. How could I have kept the business going if all my clients had discovered that, in reality, I'd spun a finely meshed web which would one day be so extensive and fragile and have so many loose ends that it was doomed to unravel?

At any café gathering, several of those seated round the table might be my clients, but each thought that he or she was the only one, at least in the early years. They thought I was monogamous, and I've always considered that a peculiarly amusing aspect of my unusual trade. To begin with none of my customers had the slightest inkling that I was really highly promiscuous. I sometimes felt like a polygamist who enjoys the favours of several wives simultaneously. I knew about them and they knew about me, but they knew nothing of each other.

If six or eight of us were in company, possibly three of those present might have bought a plot or two from me. But each thought he enjoyed a special relationship, and so they maintained their respect for each other. This was what they lived for. Many of them had already lost their self-respect. In those days, lack of self-respect was so rare that I noticed it; maybe today it wouldn't stand out so much. Self-respect is the name of a mental state that is less and less in evidence. And certainly as a virtue self-respect has gone completely out of fashion.

Naturally no one announced that next month they were publishing a novel based on an idea they'd bought from me. But, on the other hand, I several times sensed a certain nervousness that I might suddenly forget myself and blurt out, for example, that Berit's critically acclaimed detective story was built on a six-page synopsis I'd sold her for four thousand kroner. I could detect such nervousness in an overstrained laugh or a tendency towards abrupt or over-frequent digressions.

While we sat in the Theatercafe celebrating Karin's success in winning a prestigious award for her latest novel, she spent the entire evening following me with her eyes. She was ill at ease. I, on the other hand, was feeling marvellous. In the citation they had specifically remarked on the elegant construction of the narrative. Quite right, I thought. I was satisfied with Karin. She'd taken good care of what I'd entrusted to her, she hadn't buried her talent.

I wielded considerable power in such company, and that was fine by me. I could see nothing wrong in feeling powerful. Power doesn't have to be abused, and I was a good example of that. I had shared my own power with others. I'd always been excessively well endowed with imagination, so much so that I'd even begun to organise a major power distribution. Bold it may have been, brazen too, but principally it was generous. As far as the media were concerned it was Berit who had power and I who was weak. If I'd been longing for a spot in the media limelight I would have been a self-sacrificing person. But I've never wanted a place in the public eye.

It amused me to see what my authors made of all the ideas I fed them, that was all. I had a function, and so I had to function. I had to have something to live on as well, I had to ensure my cut of the profits of an industry that was becoming ever more dependent on my efforts.

When the results were tolerable, I had the pleasant feeling of being surrounded by my own pack of writers. I could feel like a king in an enlightened autocracy. I was a passable chess player, but I was even better at playing with living pieces. I liked pulling the strings, and I found it entertaining to watch how the proud authors put on airs. It was fun to watch them disporting themselves.

Even though I wasn't listed in any professional register, I decided my business deserved a name. So one day I wrote 'WRITERS' AID' on the large binders of notes I'd sold. It was a good name.

My business was dependent on bilateral contact with

authors both at home in my flat and in town. I had to cultivate the art of having several best friends at once. This led to many invitations to parties and weekend jaunts, far too many.

Once contact had been established I never needed to push new products on to my clients. As soon as they required fresh material, they would return of their own accord, come back to Uncle Petter. So they would get more and more dependent on my wares. Some stopped thinking for themselves altogether once they saw what I could supply from my own kaleidoscope of clever ideas, it was as if their brains had been sucked out. They claimed they felt quite empty.

Making people dependent on me gave me no pleasure, but it was the way I made my living. I lived by hooking fish with my bait. I wasn't selling hash or acid, nor yet cheap cigarettes or smuggled booze. It was imagination, harmless imagination. But it was the key to urban esteem, the key to something as complex as a post-modern identity.

If I came across a needy customer – at a large party, for instance – he would draw me into a corner, out into a lobby or even sometimes into the lavatory. There he would glance nervously this way and that before gabbling out his errand in a low voice: 'Have you got anything, Petter?' Or: 'Have you got anything today?' Or even: 'What could you give me for a thousand kroner?'

Both in terms of genres and price categories I had plenty to offer. A simple bit of inspiration or a pep-talk was clearly in a totally different price class from, say, the complete outline of a longish novel, or a highly detailed film synopsis. I sold half-finished poetry too, as well as quarter-written short stories. Once I wrote a complete short story which I chopped into three parts and sold to three different writers. This wasn't to milk the market for money, but simply for amusement's sake.

Quite often I'd knock together a theme with a particular customer in mind. One such tailor-made plot was sold for a goodly sum to the young man I'd met at Club 7 several years earlier and who'd already achieved a certain success with the notes I'd entrusted to him on that occasion. Like many others, he'd been influenced by the Hippie movement and the Beatles' interest in Eastern mysticism – and he was an anthroposophist to boot. I found it fascinating that he was also well versed in philosophical materialism from Democritus, Epicurus and Lucretius to Hobbes, La Mettrie, Holbach and Büchner. He confided to me that he'd got nothing to work on just then, but that he was using the time to study the *Bhagavadgita* in his quest to find a possible bridge between the materialistic and spiritualistic philosophies. The plot I worked out especially for him revolved around such questions. I gave it the working title *The Souls' Constant*, and the idea, briefly, went as follows:

The spiritualists turned out to be right in the end, and so too did the materialists. Dualists and supporters of reincarnation also had cause to pour themselves a little celebratory drink.

When the population of the world had stabilised at around twelve billion, a strange child was born in a small Bolivian mountain village on the shores of Lake Titicaca. Pablo, as he was called, was an uncommonly good-looking, but otherwise fairly ordinary, male infant. He cried like most babies, had all the natural instincts and was more than age appropriate when it came to language development and motor skills. But gradually, as he grew up it became clear to those around him that the boy had no spiritual capacity. He was subjected to several neurological examinations all of which corroborated the fact that he wasn't suffering from any physical brain damage, nor any sensual disturbance. He even learnt to read and reckon faster than most of his peers. But he had no soul. Pablo was an empty husk, a pod without fruit, a jewel box without a jewel. It would be misleading to say he had 'underdeveloped spiritual faculties' – a phrase that in any case has a strong ideological bias, as it implies that spiritual faculties are things that can be 'developed' in the same way as physical or other mechanical processes. Pablo's scourge was that he didn't have any spiritual faculties at all, and as a result he grew up like a human animal completely bereft of conscience or consideration for others. He even lacked any interest in his own welfare, living instead from moment to moment like a minutely programmed robot.

From the tender age of eighteen months, Pablo had to be put on a lead, much to his parents' despair. The village priest insisted, however, that he be allowed to go to school like other children. So, from the age of six he was transported to and from school in a pickup truck, and in the classroom his harness was fastened to a stout desk that was bolted to the concrete floor. This caused him no concern as he was completely incapable of feeling any shame or self-contempt. Pablo was almost frighteningly quick to learn, he had an impressive memory, and one of his teachers soon began to refer to him as a child prodigy. But as the years went by it was firmly established that he had no soul. It was the only thing wrong with him.

A few seconds after Pablo came into the world, a similar child was born right in the heart of London, a girl named Linda, who was also unusually pretty. In the minutes that followed, a soulless child was born in the little town of Boppard on the left bank of the Rhine, another in Lilongwe, the capital of the African state of Malawi, twelve in China, two in Japan, eight in India and four in Bangladesh. In each case it was years before the local health authorities managed to isolate this rare syndrome. As a result, the label 'brain damage' was applied, but some professionals discussed this term at length because these soulless children were often of above average intelligence.

When Pablo was twenty and already responsible for a number of murders and crimes of violence, including the brutal axe-murder of his own mother, the WHO published an international report that covered all 2000 incidences of what was tentatively called LSD, or 'Lack of Soul Disease'. The most striking thing about this UN report was that it established that LSD children were always born in tight time clusters. Roughly half of the more than 2000 reported cases had been born in the space of less than a day, and there was then a gap of four years before another 600 LSD children were born, also in just a few hours, and then fully eight years passed before there was a new wave of about 400 cases. So, as regards their time of birth, the LSD children were closely connected, but there was no geographical link between the events. Only seconds after Pablo was born in Bolivia, Linda came into the world in London, and since then there had been no further reported cases of LSD either in London or Bolivia. This ruled out any reasonable chance of contagion, and genetic causes could also be excluded. Certain astrologers were quick to interpret the LSD children as the ultimate proof of the influence of the stars, but this was soon shown to be a rash and over-hasty conclusion.

Using advanced demographic statistics, a group of Indian scientists was able to come up with the elaborate finding that LSD children were always born after the world's total population had topped a certain figure a few months earlier. After a fatal epidemic, a major natural catastrophe or the outbreak of a particularly bloody war, it always took some time for any more LSD children to arrive, and the conclusion of these Indian researchers was perfectly clear: there was a certain number of souls in the universe, and everything pointed to the figure being twelve billion. Each time the world's population passed that number, there would be a new boom of LSD children that would continue until the population figure again fell below twelve billion incarnated souls.

This new information rocked the entire world and naturally enough gave impetus to radical new ideas on the most diverse of subjects. It is to the credit of the Roman Catholic church that it almost immediately adopted a completely new attitude to a list of hoary old chestnuts, for example the official ban on contraception.

The pope and his curia were soon supporting an international movement which occasionally aired its objectives using the simple slogan: 'Make love, not worms!' The church was also categorical in its refusal to baptise LSD children. Such a thing would be as blasphemous as trying to christen a dog.

Criminal law had to break new ground as well. In certain countries LSD criminals were punished like other felons, but most societies had long since acknowledged that an LSD sufferer was no more responsible for his actions than a tidal wave or a volcano. Discussion also raged regarding the moral right of society – or the individual – to kill LSD children once a definite diagnosis had been established. Unfortunately, it was not possible to demonstrate LSD using amniocentesis. Absent attributes of the soul have nothing to do with genes.

During the past couple of years some of the oldest LSD children have been brought together to see how they would react to one another, and amongst the first were Bolivian Pablo and British Linda. As soon as they were introduced, and divested of their harness and leads, they pounced on each other and began to make love so violently and brutishly, that for the next few hours they made the Kamasutra look like a Sunday school outing. Pablo and Linda had no soul they could devote to one another, but they were man and woman and all their carnal instincts were intact. They felt no bashfulness or inhibition, because without souls there was nothing that could tame or control their lust, let alone place it in a wider context.

The meeting between Pablo and Linda resulted in pregnancy and childbirth, and the remarkable thing was that their child was a perfectly normal girl with a soul as well as a life. But as people said: what was so remarkable about a vacant soul entering a child of soulless parents? Wasn't that just what one would expect? The only thing needed to create a complete human being was that one of the universe's twelve billion souls should take up residence in a foetus. The cosmic balance was now out of kilter because for short periods there was less supply of souls than the literally crying demand.

Pablo and Linda's daughter was christened Cartesiana after the French philosopher René Descartes, because she'd demonstrated to the world once and for all that the soul was not a corporeal phenomenon. The soul is not hereditary, of course. Our physical characteristics are what get handed down. We inherit half our genetic material from our mothers and half from our fathers, but genes are entirely linked to human beings as biological creatures – human beings as machines. We don't inherit half our souls from our mothers and the other half from our fathers. A soul cannot be split in two, and neither can two souls be united. The soul is an indivisible entity, or a monad.

It wasn't the first time parallels had been drawn between Western philosophers like Descartes and Leibniz and Indian schools of thought such as the firmly dualistic samkhya philosophy. As Plato and various Indian thinkers had pointed out two and a half thousand years earlier, the soul was incarnated and reincarnated in an endless succession of human bodies. When all the universe's souls inhabit the physical world at the same time, there's a complete incarnation stoppage – until, once again, more human bodies die than are created.

Cartesiana, who was a little ray of sunshine, was immediately taken in hand by the Child Protection Agency on the grounds of anticipated parental neglect by her biological parents. Neither her father nor her mother took any notice of this, and they were allowed to stay together. Many people were bigoted enough to believe that it would be grotesque and unethical to allow more LSD people the chance to have children. At the instigation of the church the majority of them were therefore forced to undergo sterilisation.

One aspect of this story was that, from then on, people had a deeper respect for each other as spiritual beings. One didn't succumb to cursing or abusing a soul that one might possibly meet again in a hundred, or a hundred million years' time.

After the last outbreak of LSD the world's population has remained at well below twelve billion souls, but not everyone has been pleased with this development. There is a point of view that holds that a few thousand LSD children ought to be kept apart in large camps or body-plantations to provide a steady stream of organ donors. Others have emphasised the value of keeping a number of soulless Aphrodites and Adonises in public brothels for the entertainment of those who live in enforced celibacy.

The proportion of humanity that believes we ought to increase the planet's population to over twelve billion again, is only a few per cent at the moment.

In order to attract new customers I might hand out flights of fancy like this, without even necessarily demanding payment for such bagatelles. After all, food manufacturers had begun to offer an appetising tasting or two in the shops. I could recoup the money I reckoned the customer owed me when he or she returned to ask for a more elaborate synopsis.

I would pen outline ideas for a book project on a scrap of paper or a napkin and give them away to authors or deserving writers, in exchange for nothing more than the taxi fare home. For the price of a taxi to Tonsenhagen I bartered the following brief project description on the back of a restaurant bill: *Children's book (approx. one hundred pages) consisting purely of questions, ordered by category and subcategory.* That was all, but it was enough to set racing the pulse of one individual notoriously bereft of imagination. This chance client claimed that I'd given him a brilliant idea. I had specified it was no ordinary general knowledge book he was to produce. The whole idea was that the children he was writing for should be able to work out the answers for themselves. 'You must spend at least a year on the project,' I said as I got into the taxi, 'that's a stipulation.' I knew he was thorough. I knew he wasn't a fast thinker.

On several occasions I'd thrown together some tit-bits that had been lying around for years and assembled them into large miscellaneous lots – for example, a collection I entitled *Twenty-six Allegories from A to Z*. It earned me 10,000 kroner. I didn't think that was too much to ask for a pile of notes quite sufficient to launch a literary career.

One relic from the days when I'd constantly had to empty my head of voices was *Fifty-two Dialogues*. This, too, was virtually an entire writer's pack which I sold for 15,000 kroner. It was cheap at the price. Two of the dialogues have subsequently been broadcast as radio plays, one was recently staged at the principal theatre in Bergen, and I've seen three others in printed form as literary dialogues. Of course, it goes without saying that the dialogues had been somewhat polished and extended. One of them was a lengthy conversation between a pair of Siamese twins, which particularly played on the use of the pronouns 'I' and 'we'. These Siamese twins had been something of a medical sensation, as they'd lived joined together until they were over sixty years old, but the years had given them almost diametrically opposite views of life. As I worked on the dialogue, I'd toyed with the idea of giving one of them LSD syndrome, as it would have made them so much easier to tell apart, but the whole point was that this one piece of flesh was inhabited by two individual souls. Dizzie and Lizzie were two completely autonomous minds doomed to share the same body. Sometimes they would argue loudly and furiously, often ending up in a mood with one another for days on end – it would make them sleep badly at night as well – but they never injured each other physically.

If I thought a writer had the tenacity to sit for years

working on a monumental novel of, say, 700 to 800 pages, I could provide a detailed synopsis covering up to thirty sides. I sold one such exposition for 20,000 kroner to an author who was already well established. I gave the synopsis the title *The Little Human Race*. In extremely abbreviated form some of the elements it contained were as follows:

The feared Amazonian virus (which probably originated in a colobus monkey) has practically depopulated the earth, and mankind now consists of just 339 individuals. Contact between them is maintained with the help of the internet.

The whole of humanity is on first-name terms. At the present time there is a colony of 85 people in Tibet, 28 on a small island in the Seychelles, 52 in northern Alaska, no fewer than 128 on Spitzbergen, 11 in what was Madrid, a family of 6 in London, 13 in the Chilean mining town of Chuquicamata and 16 in Paris.

The majority of the survivors live in pretty isolated spots like Tibet, Alaska, Spitzbergen and a small island in the Indian Ocean, clearly indicating that they've never been in contact with the infection. But the fact that there is also a handful of survivors in Madrid, London and Paris must demonstrate the probability that at least a few have effective antibodies. It's also possible that there are other contingents of people who haven't yet managed to make contact with the world community, and even one or two isolated individuals (who might perhaps be tracked down during the course of the novel). The survivors have christened the virus that practically destroyed the entire human race The Amazon's Revenge, because it has been linked to man's insane destruction of the rain forest. Now man himself is a threatened species.

The professional and intellectual resources of the survivors are limited. There is a total of eight doctors of whom one is a neurologist, one a heart specialist and one a gynaecologist. In Paris there is an eighty-five-year-old woman who, prior to the epidemic, was one of the world's leading microbiologists, and is now the only one. There is a former professor of astronomy in Alaska, Spitzbergen boasts a glaciologist and no less than four geologists, including a brilliant palaeontologist.

After a quarantine period of thirty years during which there has been no physical contact between the colonies, the experts agree that the world is again ready for migration. Alaska, Spitzbergen and Tibet can survive isolation for two or three generations, but in order to avoid the negative effects of in-breeding, it is a pressing matter for some of the smaller colonies to get access to new blood from outside their respective reservations. There are reports from London of a father who, in desperation, has found it necessary to make his own daughter pregnant in an attempt to prevent the colony from dying out.

Large parts of the world's road network are still intact and there are several hundred million cars, of which a large proportion are almost certainly serviceable. On runways the world over there are thousands of planes ready for take-off. The little human race also has unlimited oil reserves, but there is only one aircraft technician left in the world and he lives in Tibet, and just two pilots, one in Alaska and the other in Longyearbyen on Spitzbergen. Satellite pictures show that some of the world's cities have burnt down, but that most stand as they did thirty years ago. Farm animals have largely, but not entirely, died out. In addition, the environment on earth is improving rapidly. The ozone layer is almost completely repaired, and the weather on the planet is more stable than it has been for many decades.

It is on to this stage that you make your entrance as an author. How does man's second colonisation of the planet turn out? What happens during the first wave of settlement? What challenges does the individual face? In short: what is it like to belong to the little human race? Is it liberating in any way?

You must choose which episodes you want to depict. The possibilities are endless; the only limits are set by your own imagination.

It might be wise to give names to, and describe more closely, all 339 survivors, even if you don't manage to include every one in your story. It is these 339 human destinies that comprise your material.

What was the experience, on an individual level, of the epidemic that wiped out almost all the people on earth? Which of their nearest and dearest has this or that character lost, and how did it happen? Don't forget to describe the most dramatic and gripping moments. Bear in mind too, that all the survivors have faced the fact that they would in all likelihood fall victim to the disease.

How does the individual manage now? Which siblings have found it necessary to procreate together to prevent the race dying out? What is it like for a father to make his daughter pregnant? What's it like for the daughter?

One significant challenge will be to explain how people keep in contact across the continents. Dwell on the first contact, the break-through itself – for example, between the people in Alaska and those in Tibet. What sort of equipment are they using? What are the energy resources in the respective colonies? If possible, check this with engineers and computer experts.

Will you opt for a small number of central characters around which to spin your novel? Or will you develop it episodically with a bigger cast? Bringing all 339 characters into the novel's plot needn't make it tedious provided they are clearly and sharply drawn. It may even help to give the narrative a monumental feel.

The questions are legion, and the answers are up to you as author and God. Tell all the stories, but don't lose sight of the overarching dramatic idea, the very direction and motor of this epic tale. When finished, the readers should be sitting with tears in their eyes because they must let go of all the characters they've lived with for weeks or months and with whom they now feel a strong bond.

Perhaps the material will force you to write several volumes. No matter what, don't fall for the temptation of writing too little. You and only you hold the key to the second great chapter in the history of mankind.

Don't lose sight of the almost indescribable joy that now accompanies every new child that's born. When you finish your story, several generations will doubtless have come and gone, and perhaps the world's population has increased manyfold.

Or you might choose to let the human race die out. That is your prerogative. What goes through the mind of the very last person on earth? He or she is now quite alone in the cosmos . . .

Finally, a piece of advice: don't write a word before you've read the Icelandic Sagas. And a saying: You'll forge your own path as you tread it.

Good luck!

I would rapidly form an idea of what the individual wanted – I mean what they were willing to pay for – but I also had to evaluate carefully which notes this or that person was capable of working on. Above all I had to ensure that I didn't cast pearls before swine. If a bad writer was let loose on a Rolls Royce of a synopsis, it would be like throwing it in the dustbin. People would quickly smell a rat, too. I'd learnt this way back when I was building up Homework Help; I couldn't give a B–A answer to a typical D pupil. So it wasn't simply a question of how much money a customer had to spend. Rather, I had to weigh up the quality of the material for sale against the quality of the writer I sold it to. Writers' Aid was a differentiated institution.

In certain circumstances I might even part with valuable notes for rewards other than money. If I was fond of a female writer, she might get something to write about in return for nothing more than a good time. I considered that generous, as the woman was spared the feeling that she'd had to buy something from me for money. 'You can take this idea,' I might say, 'just take it away with you, but in that case you'll stay an hour longer?'

Women are much better at exchanging gifts and services

than they are at doing business. They often turn very affectionate after receiving a good, ready-to-go outline for a play or a novel. It doesn't matter if they're married or otherwise attached – prospects of power and fame have always made women randy and ready for love.

Even in cases like these, the authors could most certainly be counted on to be discreet. Women have an impressive ability to conceal the fact that they use sex as a bartering tool. It wasn't just I who sold something to the women, it was every bit as much the reverse – it was they who sold themselves to me.

I'd ceased picking up girls on the street. I thought I'd outgrown that. But it was great to have recourse to an amorous interlude without having to mix it up with all sorts of sentimentality. A little love was nothing to get worked up about.

★

An important segment of the market was authors who'd published a novel or a collection of short stories six or eight years before, but had produced nothing since. They were the frustrated. They often continued to move in literary circles. Some had assumed a dejected mien, but as soon as they had access to a thoroughly worked-up novel synopsis, they soon brightened up and were generally willing to pay handsomely. In the worst cases, I would often include a ready-written draft of the first four or five pages just to get them going and on the right tracks.

Another group was authors who wrote well, who had a finely honed style, but who were still frustrated because they had nothing to write about. This was the group I liked working with best. They required so little – and I couldn't allow myself to go too far anyway. I couldn't just hand out a sheaf of notes that was positively bursting with narrative imagination or bubbling with perceptive insight to someone who was known for his solid character depictions, and leave it at that. But something to narrate – a story, an intrigue – could help this kind of author scale new heights. Some of them were said to have had 'a breakthrough' in their authorship. I like the word. There is something wonderfully liberating about things beginning to happen, something exploding and suddenly breaking through. Often all that's required is a pinch of dry gunpowder.

One particular reason I liked the people in this group was that they usually took good care of what I entrusted to them. They didn't hurry or waste what they'd been given to manage. Maybe they weren't exactly great writers, but they were good craftsmen, they were wordsmiths. Writers' Aid went hand in glove with this group. Here one could really talk about a genuine symbiosis. It's undeniable that my authors had an ability that had missed me out completely: they had the serenity of mind to sit down and work on a single novel for two, three or even four years, and they did so with the greatest pleasure, not to mention enjoyment. They were frequently aesthetes to their fingertips. They loved embroidering with language, doing intimate character descriptions and dwelling on all their characters' sensual perceptions. As far as I was concerned a lot of this exquisite literary inlay seemed rather artificial and fussy, if not down-right feigned and false. In contrast to such pretentious sensualism, I for my part found it hard enough to concentrate on the plots, and they weren't something I'd constructed or invented, but were more like a flock of birds I simply opened my arms to and embraced with great enthusiasm.

It was here, in the tension between the spontaneous and the elaborate, that the real symbiosis between authors and

Writers' Aid lay. I gave birth to the plots in my imagination in a totally natural way, when I was out walking for instance, and then the literary artists could painstakingly colour them in. They were far better at it than me anyway.

Although what each one could achieve was limited, there were lots of them, many working at once, and all for me. I liked the thought that perhaps there wouldn't be any stories left to tell after my mortal span had ended. I would have used up all the fireworks, I would have set them off all at once. After me, silence would reign. There would be no more to think about, there would be nothing left to ponder. I was at the controls of a mighty machine, I was arranging the greatest literary festival of all time, and I was doing it in total secrecy.

A third group of customers comprised those who hadn't published anything at all, but who were convinced they were destined to be authors all the same. This was initially the single largest group, and its members weren't frustrated. They had fame in their sights and were giddy with expectation. They were potential literary debutants. They only became frustrated when they realised that they'd paid through the nose for a substantial synopsis they could never make anything of. And so my invisible hand helped to uncover many a self-delusion. I thought this a valuable service as well. Revealing people's flights from reality can be a good deed. Writers' Aid acted to a large extent as a catalyst for self-perception. I had to wipe away many a tear. I found good use for my psychological talents.

I've always considered myself a tolerable psychologist. A knowledge of people is obviously the most important thing for a psychologist, and I felt I'd had a lot of experience, especially after visiting all those theatres and cinemas at an early age. In addition, I'd learnt a lot when I'd flown over the city and peered in through the windows at domestic life.

I'd looked in on my fellow countrymen, and not everyone can boast of that.

A psychologist must also be able to comfort, and this was something I mastered with time. To comfort is not to be stuck for words, and in a way that's close to giving free rein to one's imagination. When Calvero comforts Terry at the beginning of *Limelight*, he uses his own wealth of attitudes and outlooks. Calvero is a drunkard and a failed clown, an excellent combination in this context. As a rule it's easier to comfort another human being if you've been through the deepest despair yourself.

Terry is lying on Calvero's bed with her long, dark hair spread out over the white bedclothes. The doctor has gone, and now she comes round after her attempted suicide. Calvero turns towards her and says: *Headache?*

Terry: *Where am I?*

Calvero: *You are in my room. I live two floors above you.*

Terry: *What happened?*

Calvero: *Well, I came home this evening and smelled gas coming from your room. So I broke in the door, called a doctor and together we brought you up here.*

Terry: *Why didn't you let me die?*

Calvero: *What's your hurry? Are you in pain?* (Terry shakes her head.) *That's all that matters. The rest is fantasy. Billions of years it's taken to evolve human consciousness, and you want to wipe it out? What about the miracle of all existence? More important than anything in the whole universe. What can the stars do? Nothing, but sit on their axes. And the sun — shooting flames two hundred mega thousand miles high — so what? Wasting all its natural resources. Can the sun think? Is it conscious? No, but you are.* (Terry has fallen asleep once more and is snoring loudly.) *Pardon me, my mistake!*

Several times, later in the film, Calvero has to struggle to ignite the flame of life in the unhappy ballerina who is still in bed with paralysed legs, and on one occasion he says: *Listen! As a child I used to complain to my father about not having toys. And he would say:* (Calvero points at his own head) *This is the greatest toy ever created. Here lies the secret of all happiness!*

These potential debutants often harboured unrealistic expectations of what Writers' Aid could do for their prospective literary careers. Once they got hold of a fine novel outline, they imagined that the rest would be a piece of cake. It's nothing of the sort, of course. Having a good idea isn't enough, not even a detailed and well-constructed synopsis. Perhaps the synopsis shouldn't be too detailed, shouldn't be too tightly worked. You also need the ability to tell the story right through, to establish a plausible narrative voice and to master a few elementary stylistic tricks. Even so, it isn't here that the problems usually lie. If one hasn't learnt to write after twelve years' schooling, it's never too late to go on a writing course. There are many writing courses, there's plenty of demand for them. The shortage is in having something to write about, and that can't be taught in schools. There is no course in finding something to write about. But I was there, and this want became my niche.

Many beginners lacked something as fundamental as experience of life. It's a post-modern misconception that you can write first and live later. But many young people want to become writers mainly because they want to live like writers. This is putting the cart before the horse. You must live first, and then decide if you have something to say afterwards. Life itself is the determining factor. Writing is the fruit of life. Life isn't the fruit of writing.

In order to run Writers' Aid as efficiently as possible, I once put together some instructions which I called 'Ten tips for the aspiring author'. I wasn't some common-or-garden schoolteacher. I considered it beneath my dignity to keep on repeating myself. So it was better to stick some standard letter into the hands of any of my clients who clearly stood in need of it. This was also done in full confidence. I specified that the ten tips had been written for the recipient personally and that, naturally, they weren't to start flashing a private letter about at the university or in town. The letter's heading wasn't 'Ten tips for the aspiring author', but 'Dear Anders' or 'Dear Anne Lise'.

Gradually, as I also assumed a certain pastoral responsibility for those who had no future as authors, I had to give some thought to that too. Lots of young people had to be debriefed. This was why I wrote 'Ten tips for those who have chosen not to become authors'. That, too, was a choice worthy of respect. I'd faced it myself. The first paragraph began: *It is possible to have a completely fulfilled life on a planet in this universe without being a writer. You aren't the first who has had to look about for other work.*

I never tried to ingratiate myself with great writers. When a great writer has nothing to say, he does something else, like chopping firewood. A great writer doesn't try to find something to write about, he only writes when he has to. I was no great writer. I've always had the need to unload my thoughts, and so have had to live with a kind of mental incontinence, but I've never felt forced to write a novel. Nor, for that matter, have I ever chopped firewood.

Whenever I was recruiting a new client, I always proceeded with the greatest circumspection. I had to avoid reaching the stage of revealing that my object was to sell the author a literary idea, before he or she had a chance to retreat. I had to be able to withdraw my wares before it became apparent to the person opposite that we were talking about buying and selling. Like a cat, I could whip round in a fraction of a second and say that I'd only meant to ask the author for his opinion of something I was writing on my own account. True, I had said 'Would you buy it?', but I'd only meant to ask if he'd liked what I'd let him read. And so sometimes the whole thing would end up being turned on its head. All at once I'd be the one who had to sit and listen to an experienced author's comments. It was humiliating.

I was good at beating about the bush. It was something I'd perfected in the days when I tried to pick up unknown girls and get them to come out to the theatre or cinema. Beating about the bush is a type of improvised theatre, or a balancing act without a safety net. You can fall a long way, but it's an excellent method of honing creativity.

Nevertheless, sometimes my services were turned down after they'd been fully revealed. A few raised their eyebrows, a few shook their heads, and others protested loudly. It wasn't because they didn't like what I had to offer – quite the opposite, I think they liked it a good deal. They realised the value of what they might easily make their own. I could see temptation tearing away at them, even if only for an instant or two, and such moments were a delight. But in the long term such incorruptibles posed a considerable security risk to Writers' Aid.

The incorruptibles were unsullied. They had nothing to lose in mentioning my offers to other authors. Some of them needed special attention for a long time afterwards, and I cultivated this type of writer-nursing, too. But it must have been from these quarters that the first rumours of my activities arose. Presumably it was from the mouths of such blameless scribes that the term 'The Spider' began to circulate. This time it had nothing to do with the ancient piece of amber that my father and I had seen in the

Geological Museum. Twice in my life I've been nicknamed 'The Spider'. So I really must be a spider, after all.

The spider spins everything from itself. Or as the poet Inger Hagerup puts it: *So strange to be a spider with a ball of yarn inside her spinning all her days.* Not all writers do that. Some are like ants, they get bits from here and bits from there and subsequently regard what they have meticulously gathered together as their own. Critics easily fall for the temptation of believing that nearly all writers belong to this category. They'll often say of a particular book that it's 'influenced by', 'takes after' or 'is indebted to' certain works or trends, current or historical – and this, even when the author hasn't been anywhere near the books mentioned. But critics often assume that all writers are as educated and bereft of fantasy as they are themselves. The message seems to be that there are no longer any original impulses, not in a small country, and certainly not in Norway. But there was also a third category. The authors who used Writers' Aid's services were like bees. They came and drank nectar from The Spider's rose garden and gathered their raw material, but most took the trouble to build and work on what they had garnered. They digested the rose-garden's nectar and turned it into their own honey.

Certain established writers couldn't abide the idea that I might be doing the rounds of their fellows, helping other authors with good bits of literary advice. This was puritanical in my opinion. I've met authors who get worked up about colleagues taking inspiration from drinking a bottle of wine, smoking a joint or even going on a trip abroad. The most unpardonable sin in the eyes of many authors, is that tyros go on writing courses. Most authors don't admit to being inspired by anything other than themselves.

During periods of literary renaissance authors apply much of their intellectual effort to proving that other writers aren't up to scratch. At the end of the seventies it had begun to get crowded in the literary corrals of the publishing world, and once the pen gets full, the beasts begin to bite each other. When farmers produce too much butter or cereals, they dump the excess. When writers produce too many manuscripts, they begin to dump each other.

Of course, not everything I sold turned into a book, but I acknowledge my share of the responsibility for the literary inflation we witnessed in the final quarter of the last century. The cry went up that too many books were being published in Norway. So they hired a Danish critic – this too was at the end of the seventies. The Dane read through every one of that year's poetry collections and found almost none of them to be of a reasonable standard. But the problem hasn't only been the production of too many bad books, but that there's been a glut of good books, too. We belong to a word-spawning race. We produce more culture than we are able to digest.

Over the past few years we've been almost pedantically engrossed in fighting graffiti in tube stations while at the same time spending millions building a new National Library. But the national memory has been spray-painted as well. Nietzsche compared a person who has over-indulged in culture with a snake that has swallowed a hare and lies dozing in the sun, unable to move.

The age of the epigram is past. Under The Quay in Bergen they discovered a small piece of wood on which was the runic inscription: *Ingebjørg loved me when I was in Stavanger.* This event must have made quite an impression on the author, as it does on the reader 800 or 900 years later. Nowadays, this taciturn scribe would have covered the memory of future generations with the graffiti of a

400-page novel about his wretched love-tryst with Ingeb-jørg. Or he might have tortured his own contemporaries with catchy pop lyrics like *Ingebjørg was the only girl, she was the only girl* . . . The paradox here is that if, during all those 800 years, novels had been written with the same prolixity as in the 1970s, none of us would have been able to penetrate the massive literary tradition to get back to that simple, but charming tale about Ingebjørg: *Ingebjørg-loved-me-when-I-was-in-Stavanger*. This passionate story is pared to the bone, but it is still full of conjecture. The reader can guess at things. The reader has something to build on. You don't build on a 400-page novel.

Writing books had become far too easy, and personal computers didn't buck the trend. Authors who'd written in the old way, by hand or on a typewriter, thought that books written using a PC were second-class literature simply because the writing process had been made too simple. These machines were the enemies of literary art, and the demon in the machine was known as 'electronic word processing'. A related demon reared its ugly head way back in the Renaissance, when many people thought that the culture of writing was threatened by printing. Printed books could also be read, and by far more people, so it was impossible to shut one's eyes to the development. But for a long time, a printed work wasn't considered a proper book, merely a surrogate.

There was obviously a percentage of writers who got nowhere with the material I'd sold them. These inflicted a considerable amount of damage on my business, too. They had to blame someone, and now at last they'd found a scapegoat.

It wasn't only beginners who got frustrated when my synopses didn't make it as a book. Irritation ran high amongst those who'd previously published a book completely off their own bat. Publishers did a lot of weeding out of course, and in the early years I had no influence with them. The rejection rate has remained steady at ninety-something per cent. But many a project ran aground before it got that far. Some of my customers would come back to undo the deal. This was not merely childish, it was also expressly contrary to the conditions of sale, but it wasn't a huge problem. I lost my profit of course, as I couldn't sell the returned notes to anyone else, but I had little choice. The customers got their money back. My income was already substantial and I had to think strategically. I had the good name of Writers' Aid to consider.

By the very nature of the thing, I couldn't just let my customers leaf through the material I had for sale before they bought. I couldn't operate a ten-days-on-approval policy. As soon as I'd allowed a client to read the first page of a synopsis, it either had to end in a sale, or I had to withdraw the synopsis from the market. And so, once more, it was necessary to beat about the bush, and this I thoroughly enjoyed. I had perfected the art of asking a girl if she'd go to bed with me, without making her aware of what I was asking, yet in such a way that she was able to convince me that, later in the evening, she would. If not, I was the one who'd break off the tentative process.

Only when I was well established abroad was I able to permit a German or French writer to buy a synopsis which I'd let a Norwegian have a go at a few years earlier. On occasions this caused small conflagrations that I had to go out and smother, but I was good at putting out fires. Putting out fires is akin to the act of comforting.

★

An important watershed came early in the eighties when I realised that I could no longer just take a single payment for a synopsis which might theoretically end up as a best-seller. I began negotiating for part of the book's future royalties – for example, after it sold more than five or ten thousand copies. I pitched this at a level of between ten and thirty per cent of the author's royalty, depending on how detailed the synopsis was and the likely potential it had of becoming a best-seller in the hands of that writer. This change represented a considerable financial advance, and it was to turn me into a wealthy man – but it would also prove treacherous.

While I was negotiating a royalty I always carried a dictaphone in my jacket pocket. I considered it was in the best interests of the customer. A verbal agreement is obviously just as binding as a written one; the problem with verbal agreements is that they depend on both parties having equally good memories. It is here the dictaphone has proved indispensable, and there have been times when I've been forced to refer to it. On a few occasions I've also had to convince my client of my credentials by indicating that for many years I'd had a tape recorder wired to my phone. I was an orderly man – some might even have called me pedantic.

One of these frustrated individuals – we'll call him Robert – visited me once at my flat. He was ten years older than me, half Flemish, and he'd had his share of problems in the past. His literary career had had its ups and downs, and at quite a young age he'd fathered a son who had been slightly brain-damaged. Obviously, this had placed a strain on his relations with Wenche, and now she'd taken up with another author. Wenche and Robert still lived together, but because of their disabled son their existence together was rather like one of those old barometers where the man is out when the woman is in and vice versa. I couldn't tell to what extent Robert was aware of Wenche's affair with Johannes, but I knew all the details. The literary establishment was extremely transparent,

Robert was one of those I'd helped who expected me to assume more and more responsibility for all aspects of their lives. Also, his self-image was closely wedded to his literary merits. Several months earlier we'd been to the Casino and he'd spent practically the entire evening whining that his relationship with Wenche had always mirrored his own literary successes and failures. When he was lucky with a book, he found favour in the marital bed, but as soon as he got a bad review he was condemned to bedroom apartheid at home. I told him Wenche was the one with the problem, not him.

I didn't cherish such unannounced visits, I'd made that perfectly plain. I liked to clear away folders and suchlike before I let anyone through the door – the place could often be in quite a mess. But Robert was in such a state as he stood on the landing that I let him in anyway.

'What's the matter, Robert? Got bogged down again?' I asked before we went into the living-room.

He went right to the heart of the matter. 'I've got a feeling you're helping other people besides me,' he said.

I saw no reason to deny it. 'OK,' I said. 'Suppose there are lots of others who come to me. What of it? Aren't you happy with what you've got?'

I began to think of Jesus' parable of the workers in the vineyard. Robert was one of the very first I'd helped, and our terms had been clear. He didn't need to worry himself about any agreements I'd made with the other workers in the vineyard.

I sat him down in an armchair and fetched a couple of bottles of beer. Then I went to the music centre. 'Chopin or Brahms?' I enquired.

He was silent; he merely inhaled deeply a couple of times before saying: 'You said it was just me.'

I pretended to turn the matter over: 'Did I really say that?'

His shoulders twitched. They were broad shoulders. He whispered fiercely: 'I thought it was just us two, Petter.'

'Listen here,' I replied. 'You're probably referring to something I said ten or twelve years ago. Everything was different then, I'm not denying it.'

'But I thought it was just going to be us two,' he re-iterated.

I had little patience with such whinging. It was too late to complain about other participants in the greatest literary pyramid sell of all time when for years you've made yourself dependent on The Spider's largess. But ingratitude is the world's reward. No sooner had Professor Higgins taught some passing flower-girl to speak properly, than she de-manded to be allowed to fill the role of his one and only love.

'Do you think you would have liked knowing that I was supplying half the literary establishment with things to write about?' I asked him. 'Would you have entered into our collaboration then?'

He shook his head. 'No way,' he said.

'But you liked the reviews you got for your latest novel,' I pointed out, 'and Wenche did too. You got an eight-page synopsis from me, and you got it cheap. By the way, I agree with the man who said that your writing can be sloppy. You should have asked me to go through your manuscript. You know I don't charge much for a read-through.'

He drew himself up. 'Who are you helping?' he demanded.

I put a finger to my mouth. 'Are you mad?' I said.

He looked at me innocently. He obviously still thought that we shared an exclusive confidence. 'Would you have liked me to tell Berit or Johannes about you?' I asked.

'Are you helping Johannes?'

'Oh, come on, Robert. I think you're tired. Tell me your news. How are things at the moment?'

'Dreadful,' he said.

He didn't look too good. It was remarkable how grey his hair had turned over the past year. Added to which, he was the sort of man who kept a good head of hair for a long time, but then suddenly began to lose it.

'Have you told anyone about me?' he queried.

'Of course not,' I replied, which was no more than the truth. 'I'm discretion itself. I'm bilateral to my fingertips. You've got nothing to worry about there, at least not if you behave decently.'

Some weeks later he came back, unannounced yet again. I was annoyed. I found it intolerable that certain authors tried to intrude into my private life. I'd had a strong aversion to footsteps on the stairs from the days when snotty kids wanted to get me out into the courtyard to play cowboys and Indians. I could have had a visitor, I could have been conducting an interesting seminar with a woman writer. Or I could even have been sitting deep in concentration. Before visitors arrived I like to ensure that I'd shovelled Metre Man into the bedroom. Strangely enough, this was something he accepted without protest.

This time it was clear that people had been conferring. I guessed they had been talking about how I'd been doing consultancy work in a big way. I also assumed that all of the participants had denied that they were customers of mine themselves. Guesswork has always been a forte of mine. Making suppositions is akin to inventing plausible stories.

This was the first time it occurred to me that someone

might do me harm one day. I already felt pressurised enough to deem it necessary to tell Robert about the tapes. I'd also had cheques from him on several occasions and these I'd photocopied for form's sake. I told him I'd worked out a system by which my bank box would immediately be opened if anything happened to me. I reckoned that this would calm him down. At first he was exasperated and irascible. He was a large man and a good deal taller than me. I'd also been witness to his ungovernable temper on a couple of occasions. But soon the placidity of resignation descended on him, and I was pleased on his account. It's never good to live with the empty hope that something will avail when you're actually in a hopeless situation. If you find yourself in a dismal fix, clinging to unrealistic expectations that a miracle cure can make things better is only rubbing salt into the wound, and apathy is almost the better part as a state of mind. I spoke to him in a friendly and forbearing manner, yet another type of author-therapy. I said that no one would get to know about what he'd purchased from me. I poured him some liberal glasses of whisky and asked how things were with Wenche.

It was a couple of years before I saw him again. He was pale and told me he'd had writer's block. This time he wanted to try writing a crime novel, he said, and I let him choose between two synopses. It was generous of me. Robert knew that the synopsis he saw but didn't buy would immediately become worthless. It had to be taken from the file of notes for sale and put into the file of stories that could freely be used at parties. I couldn't completely cease being a raconteur, having pithy stories up my sleeve was a good advertisement.

The synopsis he took away with him was entitled *Triple Murder Post-mortem* and was perhaps loosely inspired by the Beatles' number 'Lucy in the sky with diamonds'. The notes ran to almost fifteen pages, but the story in brief was as follows:

In the Flemish city of Antwerp there lived three brothers: Wim, Kees and Klas. Wim had a large birthmark on his face and had been tormented by his two elder brothers throughout his childhood. In his early twenties he met the love of his life, a strikingly beautiful girl called Lucy, but his brother Kees managed to steal her from him just a few weeks before they were due to be married. Family unity wasn't improved when the brothers' parents died within a short time of one another. Their parents had made a detailed will, and the terms of the inheritance left little doubt that Wim had been short-changed. This was purportedly due to some chicanery by his elder brothers. Klas, who was a lawyer, had been especially instrumental in helping the old people arrange a will and, in the years following his parents' death, he'd gone about Antwerp all but bragging about the way he'd managed to twist them around his little finger.

Despite all this, Wim managed to set up as a diamond merchant and over the years became very wealthy. His great sorrow was that he'd never had a family. There were no women in Wim's life other than Lucy, and as a result he had no heir. The only thing that added a bit of comfort and delight to his existence was that he occasionally had visits from Lucy for old times' sake. As time went on she sometimes asked his advice in marital matters. Kees wasn't an easy man with whom to share both bed and board.

If their younger brother were to die before them, Kees and Klas had, in common decency, to inherit part of Wim's fortune, and when at a relatively young age he contracted an incurable disease, he stated in his will that his last wish was that Kees and Klas should open his large safe together. Rumours in Antwerp had it that the safe contained cut diamonds worth millions of Belgian francs.

Wim died a few months after signing his will in the presence of witnesses, and now Kees and Klas got together to open the safe. They took with them a prominent commercial lawyer. When, with greed in their eyes, they opened the priceless ark, there was a huge explosion which killed all three of them instantly. There hadn't been a single diamond in the safe, nor any bills or notes. Kees and Klas had inherited nothing but a booby-trap, but by way of recompense, it was of impeccable provenance and beautifully designed in every way.

The newspapers soon christened this grotesque episode 'the triple murder post-mortem', and the events had several judicial consequences. In his will, Wim had bequeathed all his remaining valuables, other than those in the safe, to Lucy, Kees' widow. But could the courts be absolutely certain that she wasn't implicated in a conspiracy with the triple murderer? There was no doubt that she'd visited Wim several times at his premises over the years, more often during his final year, and she made no attempt to deny this. Perhaps she'd also had access to the safe? The authorities also learnt that Lucy had recently consulted a divorce lawyer with the idea of filing for a separation from Kees on the grounds that theirs was a cold, dead and childless marriage.

A legal man was now appointed to look after the dead diamond merchant's interests as well. For who could be sure that Lucy alone hadn't placed the bomb in the safe after Wim died? And what had become of all his diamonds? Wasn't it odd to brand a prosperous diamond merchant a triple murderer before the matter even came to court?

A case was never brought against Lucy, but because of the nature of the evidence the court also issued an injunction against calling the deceased diamond merchant a murderer or a triple murderer. Or as the judge expressed it: 'Innocent until proven guilty!' And as he dismissed the court: 'De mortuis nil nisi bene'.

Because of the judicial sequels, all the press reports and perhaps also the loss of both husband and in-laws, Lucy decided to leave Antwerp. Just a few days before she was due to fly to Buenos Aires to live with a cousin she had there, she celebrated her thirtieth birthday, and on the very anniversary a well-dressed man knocked *at her door He gave her his card and said that he represented a large firm of brokers. He had a small suitcase in his hand which his client had asked him to deliver personally to Lucy van der Heijden's door on this date. Lucy signed the receipt and, as soon as the man had gone, she opened the suitcase. It was full of cut diamonds. There was a handwritten slip of paper with the diamonds, and on it was written: Dearest Lucy, I wish you every happiness on your thirtieth birthday. Live for us both. Your own Wim.*

★

The web had begun to alter in character. From now on its skeins were spun from client to client as well. And so it got denser and denser and more and more dangerous. Gradually, the symptoms of decay manifested themselves in four distinct groups.

One group comprised those who couldn't complete projects they'd started, and so felt they could begin to complain about the quality of the goods they'd received. I experienced plenty of these mental somersaults. They amused me. It's ridiculous to complain about the road-handling qualities of a Jaguar if the real problem is that the car has an incompetent at the wheel. The chauffeur's characteristics are what's in question, not the Jaguar's.

Another group was the incorruptibles. These authors were especially unpredictable because they had nothing to fear from a personal point of view. They were nervous too; they were uneasy lest I was aiding others. Some displayed signs of a near-paranoid anxiety that something of that sort was happening. They fished, but they had nothing but an ocean of rumour to trawl, they weren't able to bring one solid catch to the surface. These incorruptibles also suffered from the delusion that my services were highly exclusive, but this only served to make them even more wary, for who was I really helping? Could it be that new comet, that cocky young debutant who'd just run off with a prestigious literary prize?

People who owed me money made up a third group, people who weren't always willing to pay. In a few instances the sums in question were large. Neither the customer nor I liked the thought of it becoming publicly known that one of the year's best sellers was based on a set of detailed notes that hadn't emanated from the author's pen. None of us enjoyed it when I was forced to remind people about the tapes, but sometimes I felt I was driven to it. It was effective. The slapdash outward appearance of Writers' Aid made it all the more important that its contract work should be in good order.

The final group contained all the people who'd greatly benefited from Writers' Aid, both artistically and financially, but who felt themselves on shaky ground when they realised there were other victims in the web. The more they'd used my services, the further they had to fall, and the more frightened they were of losing face. They were ashamed of having accepted help, they felt disgraced for falling into the trap. It was understandable. But they were the ones who'd succumbed to the temptation to buy silk.

Even when they knew that I was operating on a large scale, several of my clients fell for the temptation of entering new contracts. They realised that the ship might be sinking, but they'd got the monkey on their backs and wanted more, more. As with all other drug dependency it was, perhaps, nothing more than putting off the evil moment. I asked one of them if he wasn't worried about being found out after his death. But he merely shook his head and told me that he wouldn't be around then anyway. I thought it a shameless pronouncement, but it was also striking. One characteristic aspect of post–modern civilisation is an almost complete lack of respect for posthumous honour. Life is an amusement park, and consideration stretches no further than closing time.

The idea that such customers might hate me was something quite different. But there isn't necessarily any inconsistency in being a heroin addict and loathing the heroin dealer at the same time.

I kept my own equanimity until one day I read a short article in *Der Spiegel* about a remarkable chess novel which had lately been published in Germany. I got a copy of the novel, read it straight through and was left deeply shocked.

The novel was based on precisely the same story I'd told Maria many years ago at Frognerseter only a few weeks before I'd made her pregnant. A number of details were different in the German version, all the names were new and the action took place in Germany, but the story itself was exactly the same as the one I'd invented – in some telling instances right down to its minutiae. The author was purportedly a Wilhelmine Wittmann, a person quite unknown to me, but of course the author's name might be a pseudonym.

Maria was the only person I'd told the chess story to, of that I was certain. It had remained unsold simply because I hadn't yet found anyone I thought was capable of doing it justice. So there were only two possibilities: either Maria had retold the story about Lord Hamilton to a third party, for example an author; or – and I found this even harder to come to terms with – Maria herself was hiding behind the pseudonym Wilhelmine Wittmann. The story was well told, I was quite pleased with the result, although for me the narrative had been almost inextricably linked with the Scottish Highlands.

This sudden sign of life from Maria thoroughly exasperated me. The synopsis for *Das Schachgeheimnis* was only one of dozens I'd squandered on Maria, and several of them had long since taken off as fully developed novels. Might there be other stories from the pen of Wilhelmine Wittmann? In that case Writers' Aid could risk ending up in really hot water.

Maria had already demonstrated that she had an impressive memory, and now she'd begun to play chess.

The Writing on the Wall

It was at this period that I began to establish myself abroad in a big way. It was high time. At home the web was becoming too intricate. Norway's population is small, but with a high proportion of writers. Soon it was very convenient to be able to make frequent trips to Germany, Italy, France, Spain and Britain.

First, I'd had to get myself a job in publishing. I'd known for some time this would be a necessary step. Many editors had long been aware that I was a useful chap who provided their authors with thoughts and ideas of various kinds, and I was in their good books. With increasing frequency I was asked to read for them, on an official basis. It made an excellent change, it felt good to have some proof that I'd earned money. I'd had quite a time trying to convince the Inland Revenue that I earned anything at all.

For a year I stood in for an editor of translated literature in one of the big publishing houses. I was one of many candidates, but I was given the job as soon as I expressed an interest. I didn't even need to send in a written application. I had a reputation and that was enough, everyone knew Petter. I was the *éminence grise* of the literary world.

It wasn't the least bit peculiar that a man like me applied for a job in publishing. It was just strange that I'd been so long about it and that, although I had no formal qualifications apart from baccalaureate, no one batted an eyelid. I was an autodidact, and I felt no shame at my lack of university qualifications, I'd simply skipped that stage. There are people who learn more from themselves than they can ever learn from others.

Happy the publisher who could open his doors to me. I would do a good job, no doubt about that, but secretly I knew that under cover of working for publishers I could make useful contacts abroad, acquaintances that would be hugely important for the expansion of Writers' Aid.

I remained with the firm for four years, but by the end of the first many key people in the large foreign publishing companies knew who possessed the best grasp of literary life in Scandinavia. My job was to seek out foreign titles that merited translation into Norwegian. It was easy. The agents knew who to contact, they jumped on to the *via mobile* between the halls at the Frankfurt Book Fair and came chasing after me. It was fun, it was pure entertainment. They kissed me on both cheeks and showered me with business cards. They knew that the titles I didn't take had little chance in the Scandinavian countries, and so I became a kind of litmus test. Before a German or Italian publisher offered a title to the Japanese or American market, they might turn to me and ask my opinion, and I would quickly report which titles I thought had a chance in the respective countries. I might provide the name of a contact, or I might put in a good word myself. I also gladly advised on reasonable contract terms. Thus, I was constantly being asked about matters that weren't strictly within my remit. While I was still an editor dealing with translated literature I'd already assumed a key role in disseminating Scandinavian literature abroad. I never said anything I didn't mean. If I informed a German publisher that a Danish or Swedish novel could become a great success in Germany, the publisher knew I'd weighed my words carefully. Weighing your words is important when you make your living in a social environment. Trust is something that is built up over time.

It caused much consternation when I knocked on the managing director's door one morning and handed in my notice as foreign books editor. But I had to move on. Since the early eighties I've been a scout for several large publishing houses abroad. As a scout my job has been to keep an eye on promising Scandinavian- and German-language titles and inform the publishers I represent as quickly as possible when I come across books that may be of interest. This provided me with a completely new platform and soon I was representing prestigious publishing firms in many countries, which I also regularly visited.

While travelling I continued to hatch out new ideas and themes for novels. When I was younger I'd enjoyed thinking while walking in the mountains or taking a train across the Hardanger plateau. Conditions were no worse while cruising at 40,000 feet on the way to New York, Sao Paulo, Sydney or Tokyo. Sketching out an idea for a novel was the work of a few minutes, and I needed something to think about – my mind was just made that way. I couldn't stare out into the aisle wondering when the cabin crew would bring round the coffee again. I had a profession that was perfect for long-distance journeys. I could be thankful I wasn't an ordinary business traveller, far less a novelist. A notebook is nowhere near as unwieldy as the manuscript of a novel or an entire computer, and it's also a lot more discreet. Hegel, in his aesthetics, emphasised the idea that the purer and more brilliant the art form, the less the physical space it requires.

My presence at book fairs and literary festivals the world over now went unremarked. I was paid to keep my eyes open. Ideally, I was supposed to know about an important novel before it was even published. But what no one could possibly guess was that in some cases I even knew about a novel long before it was written, indeed before even the author was aware that he or she was going to write it. This is naturally a fabulous position for a scout to be in and I've been a genius at placing major titles. People say I've a sixth sense.

Writers' Aid found it a great relief to be independent of Scandinavian writers for a change. I translated some of my most important synopses into English, German, French and Italian. It took a little work, but nothing insurmountable. I've always enjoyed reading literature in its original language, it's almost a must. And so, as far back as the early seventies, one of my hobbies had been learning new languages. Writers' Aid was now building up an increasing corpus of writers to choose from. An American or Brazilian author would consider it relatively safe to buy an idea from a Norwegian. I began to make a fortune.

Part of my routine was keeping in close contact with agents, publishers and writers, and soon I became a man lots of people wanted to woo. There was no shame in having lunch with me at book fairs in Frankfurt, London, Bologna or Paris. Being seen sitting next to me could be regarded as an honour. I was much sought after, my pleasant personality was no professional disadvantage, and I spent many an enjoyable evening in the company of female publishers. The only competitors in my niche were other scouts. The same best-seller couldn't be placed with both Seuil and Gallimard.

★

When I arrived at the Children's Book Fair that spring, I quickly sensed that it might turn out to be my last visit to

Bologna. On the very first morning I detected that things were not as they should be. I'm hypersensitive to friendly or hostile atmospheres and always have been.

I got talking to a French editor just after the halls opened. He'd recently had a big success with a story based on one of my synopses. The author, whom I'd met in a pub at the Edinburgh Book Festival several years earlier, had been faithful to my intentions, and the novel was stylistically elegant. He had paid a substantial advance, and I was to get five per cent of all future royalties both in France and on translated editions. The book had been awarded several prizes and had already appeared in seven or eight different languages. I had clear confirmation of these conditions on a dictaphone cassette, now safely deposited in a bank box together with a copy of his bank's payment advice. I also had an acknowledgement on a tape recorded from my phone at home in Oslo. I always readily supplied my home phone number to authors, the tape recorder was undetectable, and to avoid misunderstandings I would always recap our agreement.

It wasn't long before I was convinced that the French editor knew all about the provenance of this prize-winning novel. Could the author himself have told him? And if so: why? Had he absolutely no sense of pride?

Nothing was said directly, but from the way in which this editor began to quiz me, I gathered he had a suspicion that the help I'd given the author in this instance was nothing unusual. He was even confident enough to start asking me if I knew of anything else that was cooking. Finally, when I indicated that I wasn't comfortable with his inquisitive prattle – simply by picking up my paper cup of coffee and strolling off towards the German stands – he took me by the arm and said: 'Careful, Petter.' It was kindly said. But I don't think it was kindly meant. I interpreted his words as a threat. Perhaps he was fearful of his author's reputation – and by implication the good name of the entire publishing house.

I stood exchanging a few words with the editorial director of one of the large German publishing firms. He told me they had a particularly strong list that year. I was given a glass of spumante, but the man I was talking to had no notion that the preliminary work on two of the books we were speaking about, had been done in Oslo many years earlier. It made no difference.

I went round the book fair's halls all morning. I was working, I'd always loved such halls, they were good places to be. The halls and corridors of the big European book fairs were my personal imperial palaces, and my favourite of all was this vernal residence in Bologna. I ate better in Bologna. Bologna had more women.

I loved going from country to country in the fair's halls, greeting colleagues from every corner of the globe. Relatively few authors came to Bologna, but I saw my books on the displays. I had inspired dozens of books for children and teenagers over the years, but I was the only one who recognised my own fecundity. I loved talking to editors about the new books I'd initiated. I gave my opinion, I thought it only fair, and I wouldn't balk at tearing one of my own novels to pieces if I thought it was badly written. I might say that the author had squandered the plot, or at least could have used it much better. Then I might say in my own words what I considered to be the kernel of the novel. It was fun. Lots of editors found food for thought, for not all of them could expose a novel's underlying intrigue as succinctly as me. It was a joy. I didn't always manage to read every title from cover to cover before a book fair, but in broad terms I was able to given an account of the content of every book that, from an early stage, I'd had dealings with. I really knew my stuff. There was no doubt about that.

At this Bologna Book Fair, however, I had the feeling that something had altered since the Frankfurt Book Fair six months earlier. During the morning I greeted perhaps a hundred acquaintances. This was nothing unusual. Greeting a hundred people in the course of a morning isn't many at a book fair, at least not for me.

On this occasion I became more and more convinced that some of them were in league. Not all, of course – I noticed that as well. To include everyone I'd had dealings with over the course of the years, would have been as impossible as bringing all the forest ants together into one ant-hill. But a number of them had been conferring. That might mean time was up – my time was up.

An Italian agent grabbed hold of me and spontaneously exclaimed: 'So you *have* come to the fair this year, have you?' This was an odd question on two counts: she could see that I was there, and I'd been coming to the book fair at Bologna for the past ten years at least. A bit later I met Cristina from one of the big Italian publishing conglomerates. We'd known each other for years. Cristina had the loveliest eyes in the world and its second sexiest voice, after Maria. But now Cristina put a hand to her forehead as soon as she caught sight of me, as if I was the ghost at the feast. 'Petter!' she cried. 'Did you read that article in the *Corriere della Sera*?' She wasn't able to say more before she was shanghaied by a Portuguese I'd only vaguely met. He was new. And some sort of scout as well. My head was reeling.

OK, I thought. I should have read the article in the *Corriere della Sera*. It wasn't like me to be poorly informed, but it had been weeks since I'd last been south of the Alps. I didn't like the sudden change of tone, in the empire. There were conspirators abroad, perhaps a revolution in progress, and what happens to an emperor when there's a revolution?

I'd had enough for one day, even though I'd done no business. As I made for the main entrance, I caught sight of a Danish author who'd just managed to get a novel for teenagers published in Italian. I didn't think it particularly well written, but its plot was impressive and had been based on some notes he'd bought from me at a literature festival in Toronto. I considered a friendly nod was the least I deserved. It can be hectic at a book fair, but the Dane looked away as soon as he noticed me, it was almost as if he was surprised to see me alive. Perhaps being unwilling to look someone in the eyes isn't so odd if you think the said individual is no longer in the land of the living. It struck me, too, that it must be hard to meet an old friend's eyes just a few hours or days before he disappears – and more especially, I thought, if you foresee a role for yourself in the disappearing act. My imagination was too lively. I was in a bad mood. I'd begun to work up a synopsis for a novel about my own demise.

I went straight to the main entrance and took a taxi back to my hotel. I was staying on the fourth floor of the Baglioni. Once inside my room, I pulled the stopper off a bottle of mineral water from the mini-bar, threw myself down on the large double bed and fell asleep with the bottle in my hand. When I awoke abruptly after a long, deep sleep, I had the momentary fear that I'd made my début as a bed-wetter.

★

A few hours later I was sitting with a beer in the Piazza Maggiore. I was restless. There were publishing people at almost every café table, and I was on nodding terms with the majority. Some greeted me amicably, but this evening there were also others who didn't. I felt them staring at my back. I felt ostracised.

When I'd been in the mood, I'd sometimes come to this place to seek female companionship for the evening. Either with someone I already knew well or a woman I'd just been introduced to. There were no husbands or wives at a book fair, and although at Bologna both sexes were probably evenly represented, there wouldn't be a single spouse. I always took a double room at the Baglioni. Many editors and agents lived far more modestly.

I caught sight of Cristina, she was sitting with Luigi outside a neighbouring café. Luigi wasn't merely a brilliant publisher in his own right, he was also the son of the legendary Mario. Once, when in Milan, I'd been lent Mario's box at La Scala, where I'd watched a passable performance of *Turandot*.

As soon as I noticed Luigi at the adjacent café, I began thinking about my mother. She would have loved sitting in Mario's box at La Scala, she would have behaved like a queen. But I'd sat in the box alone that evening. If my mother had lived perhaps Writers' Aid wouldn't have existed, and presumably then I'd never have met Mario, either. If my mother had lived just a bit longer, everything would have been different, and perhaps Maria and I would never have met.

I began thinking about *Das Schachgeheimnis* again. Several years had passed since its publication. I'd immediately pulled the synopsis out of the binders containing notes for sale and thrown it away. What would Maria's next move be, I wondered? I felt jaded.

At a nearby table people were speaking a Slavonic language I didn't understand, but I had the feeling they were talking about me. I heard voices behind me too, and I sensed that everyone in the café was discussing The Spider. I began thinking of Hans Christian Andersen's fairy tale about the feather that turned into five hens. *Pass it on! Pass it on!* There were always rumours buzzing round a book fair, there was nothing new in that, but now they were whispering about me. I felt a prick of anxiety, I didn't know why, but I was nervous. Perhaps the thing about Hans Christian Andersen and the hard stares behind me were merely figments of my imagination. Anyone who's starting to develop a persecution complex should never stay too long at a book fair.

I decided to return to my hotel and take a sleeping pill, but then I remembered something Cristina had said in the hall. I left some money on the table for my beer and walked through the café guests towards Cristina and Luigi. They hadn't seen me. I tapped Cristina on the shoulder and said: 'The *Corriere della Sera*?'

They both jumped. Perhaps they'd been talking about me as well. Cristina glanced quickly at the clock and said she had to go. I thought it odd that she had to leave just as I arrived. Earlier in the day she'd been quick to start a conversation with a Portuguese and now she merely offered me her chair, waved goodbye and walked across the square in the direction of the cathedral. As she scurried away, she and Luigi exchanged a glance. It was as if his look said: You get off, I'll deal with Petter.

I looked at Luigi. 'What was in the *Corriere della Sera*?' I asked.

He leant back and fished out a packet of cigarillos from his jacket pocket. It was a signal that this might take a while. 'Have you heard of The Spider?' he asked.

'Certainly,' I said. 'I hear about everything.'

'OK,' he said. He took a sip of his beer. Luigi was a man of few words, he was deliberation itself.

'Was there something about The Spider in the *Corriere della Sera*?'

He nodded.

I don't think he noticed the start I gave. I tried to regain my composure.

'It's probably the first time anything has found its way into print,' I commented. 'What did they say?'

'I know the author of the article well,' he said. 'He also writes for *L'Espresso*, and he's now reportedly working on a longer feature.'

I felt irritated. I waved an arm dismissively: 'I asked what he wrote.'

Only Luigi could give just that kind of smile. 'Stefano believes The Spider is Norwegian,' he said.

'Any name?'

He shook his head. I'd started whispering. I had the feeling there were several dozen pricked ears all about us.

'He might as well be Norwegian as anything else,' I murmured, and Luigi registered the fact that I was speaking in hushed tones. 'The Spider is everywhere, he's everywhere and nowhere,' I said. 'I don't think I can help you, Luigi.'

He said: 'So, it isn't you then, Petter?'

I laughed. 'I'm flattered by the compliment,' I said. 'But as I said, I can't help you. You can tell your friend that from me.'

His eyes opened wide.

'I think you're getting things rather the wrong way round now,' he put in. 'Stefano's message to you is that you're the one who may be needing help. If you are The Spider I'd advise you to make tracks as fast as possible.'

I laughed again. I had no reason to look dejected. It was vital this conversation continue as a light-hearted chat.

I looked to left and right and whispered: 'But why? What is it this "Spider" is supposed to have done?'

He'd lit a cigarillo, and now he gave a more detailed explanation. Neither were characteristic of Luigi. 'Suppose there's a fantasy factory somewhere. Run by just one person, and let's say it's a man. He sits there covertly, constantly spinning slick story-lines for novels and plays of every kind. Suppose – strange and incredible though it may seem – he has no ambitions to publish anything himself. It's conceivable, after all. Perhaps it's an anathema to him to put his name to so much as a poem or a short story, and maybe this is because he has a peculiar desire to live incognito; but despite this he can't stop spinning tales and fables, he just can't switch the engine off. Let's assume that over the years he's built up an extensive network of contacts within the book industry, both in his own country and abroad. He knows hundreds of authors, and many of them suffer regular bouts of what we call writer's block. Assume all this, and that amongst this group of authors there are certain individuals who are prepared to ask for help. Assume now that this fantasy factory began to sell half-finished literary wares to frustrated authors. Do you follow?'

His eyes bored into mine. While he was speaking I'd beckoned to the waiter and ordered a bottle of white wine. It piqued me that Luigi thought he was better informed than me.

'Of course I follow,' I said 'and I believe you're right that something of the sort is happening. It fits in with my own experience.'

'Really?' said Luigi.

'But what of it?' I went on. 'I agree that you're describing a curious phenomenon, but don't you think writers are simply thankful for all the help they can get from this fantasy factory? Shouldn't the reading public be rubbing its hands? When the weather's damp and cold and it's hard to light a big bonfire, you're grateful to the man who's brought along a can of paraffin.'

He laughed. 'Yes quite, but I don't think you know this country too well.'

What a lame comment, I thought. I was a European after all. 'Any particular titles?' I asked.

He mentioned five novels that had appeared in Italy over the previous couple of years. Four of them were mine. The fifth, which paradoxically enough was entitled *Seta* or 'Silk', was a little gem of an Italian fable which I'd read, but which I hadn't dreamt up.

'Bravo,' I said. I don't know why I said it because it was a foolish reaction.

'By the very nature of the thing, this fantasy factory can keep going for years,' he said, 'but suppose that the writers begin to get jittery. They've become dependent on injections from external sources and now they're afraid of being caught in a dope test. At any moment, right out of the blue, they might be caught cheating. They no longer trust The Spider; one day he might strip them of all the fame and kudos their books have given them. Now, suppose that one day they get so fidgety that they begin to confer.'

Again I glanced to left and right. Was anyone listening to us? Looking round was a silly thing to do. 'Why should that worry The Spider?' I whispered. 'He hasn't done anything illegal, and I can't see that he's done anything reprehensible either. He's sure to have had clear-cut agreements with each of the authors he's dealt with.'

'You're not an Italian,' he reiterated. 'You're too gullible, perhaps. But imagine these authors owe The Spider money. Lots of money, big money.'

I hated anyone to take me for credulous. One of my greatest bugbears was associating with people who patronised me. It wasn't being unmasked as The Spider that scared me so much, but I loathed the idea of anyone thinking they'd managed to see through me.

'That's hardly a problem,' was my only comment. 'Even if he can't call in everything the authors owe him, he'll get by all the same. I still can't see why it should trouble you or me, or for that matter the reading public.'

I found it irritating that I couldn't express myself more clearly. My mouth felt as if it was full of sand.

Luigi looked me in the eyes: 'What are they planning, Petter? Think of it as fiction. Use your imagination.'

'They'll obviously try to kill him,' I said.

He nodded: 'They'll hire someone to kill him. It's not difficult in this country.'

The bottle of white wine had long since arrived, I'd already drunk more than half of it. 'Don't you think The Spider has considered that possibility?' I asked now.

'Certainly,' said Luigi, 'most certainly, just think of all the ingenious plots he's put together. For all we know he may have made use of hidden cameras and bugs, and if he's liquidated, the world may be told precisely which novels he's been responsible for. Every single sentence he's sold will be made public, on the internet perhaps, and many an author will die of shame. It may be because of all this that he's managed to keep things going for so long. The very bedrock of his business is his authors' sense of self-esteem. And anyway, a lot of good stuff has come from his direction, we mustn't lose sight of that. We may well miss him, we publishers especially.'

Now my laugh was genuine. 'So what are we talking about then? Do you really think there are people who'd be willing to murder – only to "die of shame" afterwards?'

'Oh come, come, Petter! You disappoint me. It isn't the ones who are ashamed The Spider needs to watch, he's still got a hold over them.'

Something dawned on me. I couldn't bear the thought of being considered a disappointment. I decided to repair the damage at once.

'You're right,' I said. 'Of course, it's the ones with no shame that The Spider must watch out for. Even shame fame has its own market, and it's a market that's growing and growing. When I was young, it was practically non-existent, but times change. Even the Japanese have stopped committing *hara-kiri*. It's so dispiriting, so decadent. More and more people exploit their shame. It provides them with column inches and makes them even more famous. You're right there, Luigi, your logic is correct.'

He nodded emphatically, then said: 'They owe him royalties for ever more, maybe ten, maybe twenty per cent of their own income. And these authors haven't done anything wrong either, you mustn't forget that. They won't go to prison for picking up a few ideas for a novel; but they get mean over the years, and The Spider won't be able to call in the money they owe him from the other side of the grave. Or do you think he's nominated an heir, Petter? Has he thought about that, do you think?'

No he hadn't. I'd made a huge mistake, it was embarrassing. I'd not reckoned with the shameless.

'But he still has one way out,' I said. 'He can announce that he waives his right to all monies the authors owe him. Then the danger is past, all danger is past and the authors won't have a motive for murdering him any more.'

He shrugged his shoulders. Was he smiling or wasn't he? 'I'm afraid things have gone too far,' he said. 'They say there are already plans to get him.'

Get him, get him! It put me in mind of all the times I was cornered as a child, of all the beatings I'd taken, of Ragnar who broke my head so that I had to go to Accident & Emergency and have twelve stitches.

I glanced out over the square in front of the massive basilica and soon caught sight of the little man with his felt hat and cane. The little homunculus was walking up and down the piazza lunging at passers-by with his bamboo stick as if the little thing was a rapier, but no one paid him any notice. He ought to get a grip, I thought. Metre Man was in danger of turning into a parody of himself.

Luigi appeared to have changed the subject, for he suddenly asked: 'Do you know anything about a novel called *Triple Murder Post-mortem*?'

I flinched. He must have noticed my reaction. It was Robert's crime novel which had been published in Oslo a couple of years earlier.

'There is a Norwegian novel of that title,' I said. 'I don't think it's anything for your market, Luigi.'

His laugh was almost one of resignation. Then he said: 'Oh yes, I've heard of the Norwegian version too, and that's part of the reason I'm talking to you. But I also have in mind a German novel which has recently been translated into Italian. The Italian publisher told me he was rather dismayed to discover, only a few days ago, that there is a Norwegian novel based on exactly the same story, published in the very same year as the German one. The stories are said to be so similar that there's no question of coincidence.'

I felt my cheeks begin to burn. So Maria had struck again. I tried to conceal my trembling hands from Luigi.

I remembered clearly that Maria and I had been together on the campus, it was at the time we were trying to conceive a child. We had gone out to the communal kitchen and fried some bacon and eggs before mooching back into her bed-sit and settling down on the sofa-bed again. It was then that I told Maria the story of the triple murder post-mortem. I made the story up then and there, scribbling down a few rough notes when I got home, but I hadn't given it another thought until I'd pulled it out for Robert years later. Then I'd given the story a Flemish setting because his mother was a Flemming.

'And what's the name of this German writer?' I asked.

'Wittmann,' said Luigi, 'Wilhelmine Wittmann.'

He'd stubbed out his cigarillo and now sat gazing out across the Piazza Maggiore. 'It almost looks as if The Spider has become a trifle forgetful in his old age,' he said.

He didn't know how his words rankled. I'd always exercised the greatest care to ensure that duplicates never occurred. The only person who'd had any sort of privileged position was Maria, but that was almost thirty years ago, and long before Writers' Aid had got going. We hadn't spoken for twenty-six years, and now, suddenly, she'd begun to stir. Obviously I had to make contact with her at once, it was quite unavoidable now. But then something struck me, something I hadn't realised before: I'd never asked Maria her surname. It may sound odd, but we'd only known each other for a few months, and surnames weren't much used in the seventies. The door of her bed-sit on the campus had sported a ceramic tile with the name M A R I A which she'd painted on it in large, red letters. As soon as the idea of pregnancy was mooted, she must have consciously withheld both her address and surname. I only had Maria's own word for the fact that she'd taken a job as a curator in one of the Stockholm museums. I mused at how small the world is, and yet how large a haystack when you're looking for a needle.

'So, there'll be exciting times ahead,' I remarked. 'We must keep up with developments. I'm not The Spider, but of course I'll keep my eyes open. As soon as I hear anything, I'll . . .'

He cut in: 'That's good, that's really good, Petter.'

I felt stupid. I felt tired. I'd been tired since mother died.

I looked at him: 'What shall I do, Luigi?'

'Get away from Bologna,' he said, 'the sooner the better.'

He said it with a smile, but his smile was equivocal.

I laughed. 'I think you've been reading too many crime novels,' I said.

His smile broadened. Luigi had always been a joker. Could he be bluffing when he said someone was threatening my life?

Perhaps Cristina and Luigi had guessed that I was The Spider, had taken a leap in the dark, and now Luigi was sitting there mocking me? *Triple Murder Post-mortem* could have been a title he'd got from a Norwegian publisher, or he could always have taken an option on the book, and then been surprised at how the same story had been written twice by two different authors. It wasn't even certain that there had been an article in the *Corriere della Sera*.

'You may need protection,' he said.

A bodyguard, I thought. The idea was a new and painful one.

I felt even more foolish. For once I was bereft of imagination. External pressure had laid a heavy lid on the force that welled up from within. I was empty of words. The most intelligent thing I could find to do was laugh. But it was far too cheap a reaction, and certainly nothing to boast about.

'It's no laughing matter,' Luigi said.

I was incensed. I was furious because I couldn't tell if he was bluffing. I got up and left some money on the table for the wine.

'Are you staying at the Baglioni?' he asked.

I made no reply.

'Where will you go?'

When I didn't answer that either, he stuck his thumb in the air.

'Maybe you should be a little careful with women,' he said.

'What do you mean by that?'

He grinned. 'You have the reputation of being a bit reckless. It's supposed to be your only weakness. What do you think?'

I didn't think he seriously intended me to answer. I didn't answer. He understood, Luigi was no fool. Were two men going to sit in a café discussing what they did with women? It was certainly not worth raking over, it would be too tacky for words.

'They might send a decoy. Perhaps some old girlfriend.'

I snorted. 'You read too many spy novels,' I said. I tried to laugh. I couldn't tell what he was playing at!

He handed me his card. 'Here's my phone number,' he said.

I picked up the card and read it. I can memorise numbers easily. Then I tore it up and put the bits in the ashtray. I looked into his eyes. I knew I might never see him again.

'Thanks,' I said and left, turning quickly as I felt a tear begin to squeeze out.

It wasn't the threat of a conspiracy that had upset me. Deep down I thought that Luigi had been thrashing about in the dark. He probably thought we'd be having a drink together at the fair tomorrow afternoon. But I knew that Writers' Aid was nothing more than a memory now. It didn't feel like liberation to me, more like coercion.

I walked down to the hotel feeling as if my feet had lost all contact with the ground. Perhaps the problem was that my feet had never touched the ground. I'd been on a cloud all my life, I'd been floating around on a cloud. I'd been operating as a brain divorced from everything. There had been only two spheres: the world and my brain, my brain and the world.

I'd had more imagination than the world could make use of. I'd never really lived life, I'd been compensating for it. I didn't know if I'd been punished by my mother, or by Maria or by myself.

★

I slept for a few hours and was in the hotel lobby at the crack of dawn next morning. It was quiet out in the Via Independenza, but I felt I was being watched by a young man as I checked out. He was sitting in a leather armchair, pretty well hidden behind a newspaper. It was impossible to judge if he'd just got up, or if he hadn't yet made his way to bed. When I went out into the street and got into a taxi, he followed. I didn't see him get into a car, but I believe I caught a glimpse of him again at the airport. He had an earphone in his ear, and it didn't suit him. I think I must have been quicker off the mark with my boarding card than him.

When I arrived at the gate, boarding had already begun, and just a few minutes later we taxied out and took off. I was in seat 1A, I had asked for it specially. I preferred to look out to my left. I was bound for Naples, it was the first flight from Bologna that morning. Twenty minutes later there was a plane to Frankfurt with a connection for Oslo.

As soon as we'd reached cruising altitude, I lowered the back of my seat, and an almost transfiguring peace enveloped me. Soon an episode from my childhood returned to my mind. It was a real memory, but it was something I hadn't thought about since I'd been a boy. Everything had passed so quickly, I was already as old as my mother when she died. This was the story:

I'd learnt to read and write by the time I was four. My mother didn't teach me, she thought I should wait until I started school. I learnt to read by myself, and I seem to recall that I'd pulled an old ABC from the bookshelf completely on my own initiative. I didn't consider it inordinately difficult to keep track of twenty-nine letters.

Once when I was at home on my own, I picked up a red crayon and went into my mother's bedroom. Her bedroom had two large windows with blue curtains in one wall with a fine view out over the city. White wardrobes occupied another wall, but on the other two there was nothing but white wallpaper. It was boring. I think I felt sorry for my mother. At least I had a picture of Donald Duck on my wall.

I had made up a lovely fairy tale in my head, I'd been working on it for days, but I hadn't let on about it to my mother. The fairy tale was to be a surprise. I took the red crayon and began to write on the white wallpaper. I had to stand on a chair to begin with because I needed the entire wall, I needed both walls. Several hours later I was finished. I lay down on mother's bed and read all through the long story I'd written on the wall. I was so proud, now my mother could lie in bed every evening and read the lovely story before going to sleep. I knew she'd like it, it was a beautiful story, and perhaps she'd like it even more because I'd made it up specially for her. If I'd invented a story for myself it would have been different, and if I'd cooked up a fairy tale for father, it would have been different again. But my father no longer lived at home, he hadn't done since I was three.

I lay on the bed waiting for mother. I was looking

forward to her return, I was giddy with anticipation. I'd often have a small surprise ready for her, but this was quite different, this was a big surprise.

There, as I sat on that plane to Naples, I suddenly recalled the sound of my mother letting herself into the hall that particular afternoon. 'Here!' I shouted. 'I'm in here!'

She was livid. She was absolutely livid. She was beside herself even before she'd read what I'd written on the wall. She yanked me off the bed and threw me on the floor, she slapped me hard on both cheeks, then she dragged me out into the corridor and locked me in the bathroom. I didn't cry. I didn't say a word. I heard her ring my father, and heard how she was angry with him too. She said he had to come to the flat and hang some new wallpaper. And several days later, he did. The smell of glue hung about for weeks. It was humiliating.

It was a long time before my mother let me out of the bathroom. First she had her dinner, drank her coffee and listened to the first two acts of *La Bohème*. She said I'd better start getting ready for bed. I did exactly as I was told, but I didn't utter a word. I didn't talk to my mother for several days, but I did everything she told me. Finally, she had to coax me to start talking again. I said I'd never write on the wall again nor, I declared, on paper either, not even loo paper. I was very resolute and in a way I kept my promise. After this episode my mother was never allowed to see anything I'd written, not so much as a syllable. She couldn't look at my homework either. This was sometimes brought up with my teachers, but they agreed with me. I was so good at doing my homework on my own, they said, that it wasn't necessary for mother to see my books. Quite right too.

I wouldn't go so far as to say that this event was what put me off being a writer, but it was certainly what made me stop drawing. There was little point in drawing when I had no one to show my drawings to. I think I can remember being struck once by the impossibility of checking whether mother would be able to read what I'd written if I ever published a book that had thousands of copies printed. But I was never going to expose myself like that. I'd exposed myself in my mother's bedroom, that was the writing on the wall. Mother would never get the chance to stroll into a bookshop and buy a book with my name on it.

I turned down the air hostess's invitation to breakfast and tried to sleep, but after a few minutes' doze, I jerked back into wakefulness again. I glanced down at the even Umbrian landscape. I was forty-eight, half my life lay behind me, seventy-five per cent of my life lay behind me, perhaps more, perhaps ninety per cent. Life was so indescribably short. Perhaps that was why I wouldn't put my name on a book jacket. That thin veneer of culture, of human glory and affectation, drowned in insignificance by comparison with the colossal but fleeting adventure through which I was now journeying. I had learnt to ignore the insignificant. Ever since I was a child I'd known of a timescale quite different to that of weekly magazines and the autumn's annual crop of books. When I was small, my father and I had seen a piece of amber which was millions of years old, and encased within it was a spider that was just as old. I'd been on earth before life began four billion years ago, I knew that the sun would soon be a red giant, and that long before that the earth would be a dry and lifeless planet. If you know all this you don't enrol for an evening course in DIY. You haven't the placidity of mind for it. Nor for a 'writing course' either. You don't mince about cafés saying that you've 'started writing something'. Perhaps you do write, there's nothing wrong in that, but you don't sit down to 'write'. You write only if there is something you want to say, because you have a few words of comfort to give other people, but you don't sit down behind a desk in a spiral of the Milky Way and 'write' something just for the sake of <w>r<i>t<i>n<g> or of <<w><r><i><t><i><n><g>>. But the poets posed on the catwalk. Climb aboard, ladies and gentlemen! Welcome to this season's collection from Kiepenheuer & Witsch. We have a creation here that should be of special interest to you. This is a superb Armani novel, unrivalled in its genre. And here we see Suhrkamp's lyric fashion icon – '*mit Poetenschal natürlich . . . und mit Ord und Datum, bitte!*'

I was tired. But now Writers' Aid was at an end and a literary epoch had passed. I would never again return to the big book fairs. I had decided to try to salvage my life.

When we landed at Naples, I was the first passenger off the plane. I ran through the arrivals hall, jumped into a taxi and told the driver to take me to Amalfi. He couldn't have been asked to do such long trips very often.

I'd never been to the Amalfi coast before, but over the years many people had suggested I spend a few days in that charming town on the Sorrento peninsula. Maria had spoken of Amalfi, she had once been there with some girlfriends. Robert, too, talked constantly about his trips to southern Italy, in the days before Wenche had left him.

We drove past Pompeii, and I tried to imagine the townspeople in the final few seconds before the volcanic eruption. As soon as I'd got one clear image, I'd do my best to erase it again. What I had seen could be summed up in one word: *vanitas*. Then the blow fell. Then the rage of Vesuvius poured down over all the pretentiousness.

When we'd left the mountain behind us and were driving

through lemon groves towards the coast, I asked the driver to take me to a hotel I'd heard of. I'd no idea if the Hotel Luna Convento had any vacant rooms, but Easter was still a full week away.

There were lots of vacancies. I asked for room 15, and was told it was free. I said I wanted to stay a week, and not long afterwards I was sitting in front of a window looking out across the sea. There was a pair of large windows in the room, and Metre Man was already peering over the sill of the other one, scanning the ocean as well. The sun was still low in the sky, it was only a quarter past nine.

I bent down to look at an old escritoire. Henrik Ibsen had once sat writing at this very desk. I knew that Ibsen had taken room 15 at the old inn, originally a fourteenth-century Franciscan monastery. It was here he'd completed *A Doll's House*, and now a portrait of him hung on the wall.

It struck me that I had grown up in a kind of doll's house myself. Once again I fell to thinking that there was something I was forever trying to forget, and it wasn't the fairy tale I'd scribbled on my mother's wall, but a nightmare that sat even deeper. I felt a horror of the cold, dark depths beneath the thin ice I'd been skating on.

I conjectured that it was in this room that Ibsen had taught Nora to do her wild Tarantella, which in reality had been her dance of death. Anyone bitten by a tarantula could dance themselves to death. I'd never thought of it before, but now it struck me that the spider had of course been Krogstad, the lawyer. I had to smile. I'd come to Naples quite by chance. If there was such a thing as destiny, it was certainly ironic.

I glanced down at the sea and again looked around the room. Metre Man had begun to wander restlessly to and fro across the floor's ceramic tiles. At one point he halted and inspected me with an authoritative air, thrusting his bamboo cane in my direction. '*Well, then! What now? Shall we confess our sins?*'

I unpacked my laptop, sat down at the desk and began to write the story of my life.

Beate

There are two empty whisky bottles in the corner by the fireplace. I don't know why room service hasn't taken them away, but I'll put them in the wastepaper basket before I go down to breakfast early tomorrow morning.

I've been here for ten days, and for the past three I've written nothing. There was nothing else to write. Now there is something more.

For the first time since Maria left I've met a woman who is on the same wavelength as me. I've found a girlfriend here and we go on long walks together in the hills above the Amalfi coast. She dresses girlishly in white sandals and a yellow summer frock, and she'll even venture into the hills dressed like this. She's full of humour and not the sort to run away from a cold shower. Today we were overtaken by a terrific thunderstorm.

I've thought a lot about Luigi's warning, but I can't believe Beate is a decoy of any description. We're already strongly attached to one another. If she was sent to the Amalfi coast as a decoy, she must have changed her mind since. I still haven't noticed any men with earphones and we've been up to the Valle dei Mulini twice already. There wasn't a soul to be seen.

I feel certain Beate is harbouring a secret too. Her reaction was so extraordinary when we came down from the little village of Pogerola this evening. She had a really serious anxiety attack, burst into floods of tears and said we oughtn't to see each other any more.

But tomorrow we're to walk across the hills to Ravello. Beate is unattached, perhaps I'll ask her if she wants to come to the Pacific with me. I shall inform her about Writers' Aid, I've already told her some stories. I don't need to restrain myself any more, I've de-classified all my synopses, I've taken back what is mine.

Soon Beate will be able to read everything I've written at the hotel over these past few days. I don't think my adventures with girls will shock her, maybe they'll give her a good laugh. After all the tears she's shed this evening, I wouldn't begrudge her that. I'm sure she's lived life to the full too; I haven't enquired about her past, but it's irrelevant, irrelevant to us. She still doesn't know that I'm extremely rich, but I'll ask her if she wants to come to the Pacific with me before I tell her I'm a man of independent means. I've already begun to investigate air routes. There's a flight from Munich to Singapore on Wednesday, and I've booked two seats just in case. I've booked 1D and 1G in first class.

After that, we'll see.

We could do a bit of island-hopping until we find a place to settle down. For that matter, we could buy a house. Perhaps we'll find a bungalow with a view of the sea. I'm not too young to live as a pensioner, and Beate paints watercolours.

My imagination is running away with me again. It's too fleet of foot.

★

When I'd finished writing out a kind of synopsis of my life – up to and including my hasty departure from Bologna – I sat for hours by my window just staring down at the breakers that swept into the Torre Saracena. It was Good Friday, the day before I met Beate. I didn't even go into town to look at the great procession that celebrates Christ's Passion.

I'd decided to enlist the help of the hotel staff in e-mailing what I'd written to Luigi. It might be useful to have a back-up copy somewhere remote from my own person. Luigi could, if he wished, give my entire story to his journalist friend on the *Corriere della Sera* and let him use the material in any way he chose. It was in my interests that the story was made public, or at least referred to, as soon as possible. After that I could see about getting out of the country. An outlaw shouldn't remain too long in one place.

However, when I awoke the next morning, I decided to spend a day in Amalfi before I took off. It was Easter Saturday, the weather was beautiful and I still hadn't been to the Paper Museum. After breakfast I went into the town and bought the *Corriere della Sera* as I'd done every day. A couple of mornings previously, in a brief article about the Bologna Book Fair, there had been a few lines to the effect that this year's fair hadn't produced any blockbusting title that every publisher was fighting to get an option on, there was no new Harry Potter on the horizon. The rumours this year, it said, were quite different: they all centred on 'The Spider'. This mysterious nickname was a front for a modern fantasy factory (*sic!*) that sold literary and half-finished novels to writers all over the world. The article's author, a Stefano Fortechiari, pointed out that in antiquity an influential author might be accredited with a plethora of different books which, in reality, were the works of various other writers. The fantasy factory was supposed to be the complete reverse. Several dozen novels, perhaps several hundred, were in fact based on drafts and ideas that originated from one single person. I had to smile as I read these lines. I had made my mark.

The article's author had an interesting point, but the phenomenon he was describing wasn't as unique as might be supposed. From time immemorial, churchmen had claimed something similar for the books of the Bible. The Bible originated from many different hands, of course, but theologians believed there was one all-encompassing meta-author behind the whole collection. They didn't necessarily think that God had verbally inspired every sentence in the Bible, God didn't work like that. But he'd given each of the authors a clue. He'd given each something to think about.

I had considerable collegial sympathy for the way God worked with people. He, too, laid claim to a certain recompense, he demanded everything from praise to penance. But he went further than me: he threatened to destroy all those who didn't believe in him, and modern man refuses to live under such conditions. Now God was dead and it was the frustrated and their conspiracy that had murdered him.

So, this Stefano was some corroboration that Luigi hadn't been bluffing, but it was little more than an indication. There was nothing in the current article to show that this journalist had written anything about the 'fantasy factory' before. Quite the opposite – it was almost as if the article was based on the long chat I'd had with Luigi in Bologna. Nor was there a single word in the article about either the Norwegian or Italian versions of *Triple Murder Post-mortem*.

I couldn't quite be sure if there really were any plans to kill me, but I wouldn't allow any suspects the benefit of the doubt.

I crossed the busy coast road and sat down in a pizzeria on the beach. I ordered a tomato salad, a pizza and a beer.

I had to have my eyes about me the whole time. I no longer believed that anyone had followed me from Bologna, but it wasn't inconceivable that, for example, a British or

Scandinavian publisher had combined a trip to the Book Fair with an Easter holiday in southern Italy afterwards. The Bologna Book Fair was always either just before, or just after, Easter.

While I waited for my order, I read the paper, but I also became aware of an attractive woman in a yellow dress and white sandals. She might have been about thirty and sat by herself at one of the neighbouring tables. She tried to light a cigarette with a pink lighter, but without success. All at once she got up, crossed to my table and asked if I had any matches. She spoke Italian, but it was easy to hear that she wasn't a native. I told her I didn't smoke, but just then I caught sight of a lighter lying on the table next to mine. I simply picked it up, without asking the German tourists' leave, and lit her cigarette before replacing the lighter and nodding my thanks to the Germans. When I'd eaten and paid my bill, I waved to the woman with the cigarette as I went. She sat drawing something on a sketch pad, but she gave me a serenely enigmatic smile and waved back. I was certain I'd never met her before, for if I had I'd certainly have remembered such a special face.

I walked up through the town and went into the Museo della Carta in an old paper mill. Amalfi was one of the first places in Europe to manufacture paper. An elderly man demonstrated how they pulped wood prior to pressing and drying the wet sheets. He still made paper the old way – a tradition, he explained, that went right back to the Arabs of the twelfth century. He showed me the exquisite writing paper he'd made and how a watermark was formed.

It was hot, but I was determined to take one final walk in the Valle dei Mulini before I left Amalfi. I'd been up there once before, and then as now it had been hard to negotiate the alleys that led out of town, but soon I'd left civilisation behind me.

Luxuriant lemon groves flanked the path on both sides. The trees were covered in black and green nylon netting to protect the lemons from wind and hail. I greeted a little girl who was playing with an old hula-hoop, but saw no trace of the black-clad woman who, a week before, had leant from a window and given me a glass of limoncello. The Easter sunshine had coaxed out hundreds of tiny lizards. They were extremely timid. Perhaps people didn't come along here very often.

I put the last house behind me and passed an old aqueduct. I was walking on a gravelled hiking path called the Via Paradiso, and its name was apposite. Soon the Via Paradiso had become an idyllic, riverside cattle track in the bottom of the lush valley.

The last time I'd walked here I hadn't met a living soul, but now all of a sudden I heard the sound of snapping twigs on the path behind me. Next moment she was by my side. It was the woman in the yellow dress.

'Hello!' she said, still in Italian, smiling broadly, almost as if she expected to find me here. She had deep brown eyes and a profusion of wavy, dark blonde hair.

'Hello!' I replied. I cast a wary glance down the path, but she was alone.

'It's so lovely up here,' she said. 'Have you been before?'

'Once,' I said.

Clearly she couldn't decipher that I was a foreigner. She pointed to a waterfall fifty metres ahead. Then she said: 'Shall we bathe?'

This line alone was sufficient to convince me that I'd met the woman of my life. We'd never seen each other before, she was wearing white sandals and was dressed in nothing but a thin summer frock. It was sweltering hot, neither of us looked particularly prim, but suggesting we should bathe together was very uninhibited.

Shall we bathe? The three words were pregnant with subtext. She both did and did not mean that we should jump into the waterfall together. She was saying that the sun was hot. She'd pointed to the waterfall and called it refreshing and beautiful: it was tempting. She had posed the brief question to see how I'd react. She was saying that she liked me. Now she wanted to see how I responded. She wanted to watch me disport myself. She was setting the tone, the three words were a tuning fork. The woman in the yellow dress had said that she was willing to walk with me, but that she would rather not have any heavy conversation. She was saying we had nothing to be ashamed of.

I remembered Luigi's admonition and said: 'Perhaps we could do that tomorrow.'

She had inclined her head slightly. She had been testing me and I'd given the best answer she could hope for. It was a Solomonic answer. Had I immediately ripped off my shirt and begun loosening my belt, I'd have made a fool of myself. The invitation wasn't that literal. It was a rebus. If I'd said that I never bathed in waterfalls with women I didn't know, I would again have failed the tests she'd set me. Hiding behind such general norms would have been over-starchy, it would have been a rebuff.

She proffered her hand. 'Well, tomorrow then,' she said. She laughed. 'Come on!' she said. And we began walking. She walked a pace ahead of me on the path.

Her name was Beate and she came from Munich. She'd been a week in Amalfi too, but she mentioned she was staying all summer. She painted watercolours, had rented a bed-sit from an affable widow, and was due to hold a big exhibition in Munich at the end of September. I'd have to come to Munich then, she told me. I promised – I couldn't really do otherwise. The previous year she'd had a small exhibition of scenes from Prague after spending a couple of months in the Czechoslovakian capital.

We had switched to German. It was easier for me to speak German than for Beate to struggle on in Italian. I could hear that she hadn't been born in Bavaria and thought there had to be a reason why she didn't say where she came from. I don't know where I got the notion that her parents might be Sudeten-Germans, but it was probably due to her mention of Prague.

I didn't tell her exactly what I was called, but I used a suitable pseudonym. I looked her right in the eyes as I said it. I needed to test her out. She gave not the least reaction to the pseudonym.

I wasn't a fool. Perhaps even now I was in love, but I wasn't irresponsible. I couldn't shut out Luigi's warning. She didn't ask my surname, but I told her I was Danish and lived in Copenhagen. She didn't react to that either. I told her I was the editor-in-chief of a Danish publishing company, which was quite plausible. I'd brought a laptop and some work to Amalfi, I explained. I needed to get away for a while. I thought it sounded reasonable. But I'd under-estimated her.

'Work?' she queried.

'Some editorial work,' I said.

'I don't believe a word of it,' she said. 'No one travels from Denmark to southern Italy just to concentrate on "editorial work". I think you're writing a novel.'

I couldn't lie to her, she was much too clever.

'All right,' I said. 'I'm writing a novel.' Then I added: 'I like it when you see through me.'

She shrugged her shoulders. 'What is your novel about?'

I shook my head and said I'd promised myself not to talk about what I was writing until it was finished.

She accepted my answer, but I still wasn't sure she believed me. Was it possible that she knew who I was? If Luigi's hint at an intrigue had been a joke, I'd never forgive him.

We passed the moss-covered ruins of several paper mills. Beate pointed out flowers and trees and said what they were called. We spoke about the Jena Romantics' fascination with ruins and the traditional countryside. We talked about Goethe and Novalis, Nietzsche and Rilke. We talked about everything. Beate was a fairy tale, she was a whole anthology of fairy tales. She was no straightforward type, she had a multiple personality. I felt she was like me.

It's not often I'm captivated by a woman, but on the rare occasions when I do meet a woman I fall for, it doesn't take me long to get to know her. It is those you don't like that take the longest time to know.

After we'd passed the ruins of an ancient mill called Cartiera Milano, a path turned off to the right. Beate asked me if I'd been to Pontone. I knew it was the name of a small town that lay on the saddle of hills above Amalfi, but I hadn't been up there. 'Come on!' she said and beckoned me to follow. She had a map and told me that the path was called Via Pestrofa. My inability to work out any etymology behind the name irritated me.

We put the valley behind us and joined a stone-paved cart track with high kerbstones on either side of it. We halted several times and looked down into the valley. We could still hear the deep roar of the waterfall we were going to bathe in next day, but soon its sound subsided and merged into the gentle chatter of the river that still reached us from the depths of the Valle dei Mulini.

We were short of breath by the time we got up to Pontone an hour later. We had talked continuously and we were already well enough acquainted for each to know that the other had a secret in life. I was afraid to let her know my intimacies, and she seemed just as anxious that I shouldn't begin digging into hers.

Beate had mentioned that she'd lost her mother quite recently, and that they had always been very close. She'd died quite unexpectedly. It had actually happened on her birthday, while she was at the Bayerischer Hof Hotel celebrating the occasion with some friends. Her mother had been in sparkling form, but then, just as she'd been about to go to the table with a glass of champagne in her hand, she'd suddenly collapsed. A doctor was present amongst the guests, but it proved impossible to save her life. She hadn't died of heart failure, or any other demonstrable condition, she'd simply vacated this world. 'And your father?' I asked. 'I'd rather not talk about him,' she replied rather brusquely. Then she repented and said in a milder tone: 'It can wait until tomorrow.' She looked up at me and laughed. Perhaps she was thinking about the waterfall.

Occasionally her sandals forced her to take my arm where the path was rough or steep, but as we went through the town gates of Pontone, she linked her arm through mine and like this, as if we were man and wife, we walked into the Piazzetta di Pontone. It was so easy, it was like an amusing game, it was as if we were playing a trick on the entire world. Some people take years to get to know one another, but we were in a totally different league. We had already discovered many subtle short-cuts to each other. But we respected each other's little secrets, too.

After we'd taken a look at the view, we went to a bar and stood drinking a cup of coffee. Beate ordered a limoncello as well, and so I had a brandy. We hardly spoke now. Beate smoked a cigarette – I had snatched the matches out of her hand and lit it for her. We leant on the counter looking provocatively into one another's eyes. She was smiling, it was as if she was smiling about several different things at once. I said she was nuts. 'I know that,' she said. I said I was much older than her. 'A bit older,' she said. Neither of us had revealed our age.

The way down from Pontone to Amalfi was a steep, narrow path with more than a thousand steps. At one point we passed a man leading a mule. We had to squeeze up against the rock face, and this also forced us close together. She smelt of plums and cherries. And earth.

We sat down on a bench to rest our legs. A few moments later Metre Man came along and climbed up on to an adjacent kerbstone. But first he glanced up at me and with his bamboo cane asked if it was all right to sit down. I couldn't be bothered to argue as I knew he'd do exactly what he wanted anyway. 'Metre Man is Master' was a catch-phrase he'd used constantly when I was little. I could hardly speak sternly to him while I was in Beate's company. If I'd admonished him verbally or just waved him away, she might have been scared, she would certainly have begun to doubt my sanity. I decided instead to tell Beate a fairy tale, indirectly addressing it to the little man as well. The bones of it went as follows:

Long, long ago in Prague, the capital of Czechoslovakia, there lived a small boy called Jiří Kubelík. He lived in a poky little flat with his mother. He didn't have a father, but when he was about three years old, he began to have frequent vivid dreams about a little man with a green felt hat and a reedy bamboo walking-stick. In his dreams, the little man was exactly the same height as Jiří, but otherwise he looked the same as any other man. He was just much shorter and far more glib-tongued than most.

In these dreams the little man tried to convince Jiří that it was he who dictated everything the little boy did and said, and not only at night when he slept, but during the day as well. When Jiří sometimes did things that his mother had forbidden him, he imagined that it must be the little man who'd made him do it. It happened more and more often that Jiři used adult words and expressions and his mother couldn't work out where he'd picked them up. He could also rattle off the strangest stories to her, small fragments or long narratives which the little man had told Jiři as he slept.

His dreams about the little man were always lively and amusing. And so Jiři generally awoke with a smile on his lips, and never protested when his mother said that it was bedtime. His problems began one morning when the little man failed to disappear with his dream, for when Jiři opened his eyes that sunny summer's morning, he could plainly see the man with the green felt hat in his room standing by the bed, and the next second the miniature man had slipped out of the open door into the hall and from there, into the living-room. Jiři hurriedly got out of bed and, very naturally, rushed into the living-room too. Sure enough, there was the little man, pacing to and fro amongst the furniture brandishing his cane. He was very much alive and full of vigour.

When Jiři's mother emerged from her bedroom a bit later, her son was eager to point out the little man who just then was standing in a corner of the living-room prodding one of the books in the bookcase with his cane. But his mother had honestly to confess that she was quite unable to see him. This surprised Jiři, because for him, the little man with the stick was anything but a vague or shadowy apparition. He was as clear-cut as the big vase on the floor or the old piano, which his mother had recently painted green because the original white colour had begun to go yellow.

However, certain aspects of the little man's behaviour were quite different from when he'd appeared in the dreams. Occasionally he still turned to say a few words to Jiři, but that was the exception now. This was a major shift in their relationship, for while the little man had been in Jiři's dreams, he'd played with words almost continuously. It was as if, from this time on, he had renounced almost all use of language and speech in favour of young Jiři. In the

176

dreams he had also loved picking plums and cherries which he'd put straight into his mouth and eaten with great relish, or sometimes he'd take Jirí to a secret stockpile of fizzy drinks he kept in the cellar, there to open bottle after bottle of pop which he put to his mouth and emptied before even asking the boy if he'd like to quench his thirst as well. In the real world, on the other hand, he never picked up any objects in the room – apart from his own hat and cane which, as if by way of compensation, he twirled and flourished almost ceaselessly. He didn't eat or drink anything, either. In the world of reality he remained a mere shadow of himself compared with the vitality and friskiness he'd demonstrated in Jirí's imagination. Perhaps it was the price the little dream man had had to pay for advancing from dream to reality; after all, it was a considerable leap.

Jirí got bigger, and the little man continued to scamper around him almost everywhere he went, but without growing by as much as a millimetre. By the time Jirí was seven he was already almost a head taller than the little man, and from that time on he began to call him Metre Man, as he was only a metre tall.

As soon as Metre Man entered reality and appeared in Jirí's flat for the first time, Jirí never dreamt about him again. He was sure, therefore, that he'd either escaped from the dream world of his own volition, or that he'd accidentally got separated from the fairy-tale land he came from and could no longer find his way back. Jirí thought it must be his fault that the dream man had got lost, and so he never gave up hope that one day Metre Man would succeed in getting back to the world he came from. That was where he belonged after all, and we must all be very careful not to stray too far away from the reality of our roots. Gradually, as Jirí got older, having the little man around him all the time often made him tired and irritable.

All through Jirí's life Metre Man followed him like a shadow. It might look as if he was Jirí's sidekick, but the little man always maintained that it was the other way round, that he was the one *pushing the boy, and that it was he who made all the decisions in Jirí's life. There must have been something in this, because Jirí could never control when or where he'd find Metre Man. It was always the little man who decided when he would appear. And so he could pop up at the most inconvenient moments in Jirí's life.*

No one apart from Jirí could ever catch so much as a glimpse of Metre Man, whether at home in the flat he still lived in or out on the streets of Prague. This never ceased to amaze Jirí.

One day, when he'd grown to manhood, he met the great love of his life. Her name was Jarka and as Jirí wanted her to share his life and soul, he tried to point out Metre Man on a couple of occasions when he materialised in the room, so that his love could also catch a glimpse, however fleeting, of the tiny wonder. But to Jarka this looked as if Jirí was in the process of losing his wits, and she held herself aloof from him a little. Then, finally, she left him for a young engineer, because she felt that Jirí was living more in his own fantasy than in the real world with other people.

Jirí lived out his life in loneliness and isolation, and it was only when he died that an extraordinary change occurred. From the day Jirí was released from time – by that I mean our world – rumours began to abound in Prague that people had seen a homunculus strolling alone down by the banks of the River Vltava in the evenings. Some claimed they'd seen the same manikin strutting around and excitedly swinging his little bamboo cane about him in the market-place of the old town as well. And last but not least, the little man was observed at irregular intervals sitting on a gravestone in the churchyard. He always sat on the same grave, and on the stone was carved JIRÍ KUBELÍK.

An old woman would sometimes sit on a white bench and give the little man a friendly wave on the rare occasions he took up position on Jirí's gravestone. It was Jarka who, all those years before, had turned down Jirí's hand because she thought he'd lost his reason.

Gossip had it that the old lady was probably Kubelík's widow.

Maybe that was because she was always sitting on the white bench in the churchyard staring at Jirí's gravestone, and then again, maybe not.

I spent almost an hour over the story of Jirí and Jarka and, by the time I'd finished, the little man was no longer sitting on the kerbstone keeping an eye on us. Perhaps I'd frightened him off.

Beate was looking a bit pensive. 'Was that a Czechoslovakian fairy tale?' she enquired.

I nodded. I felt no desire to tell her I'd made it up myself.

'A literary fairy tale?' she queried again.

I answered yes to that too, but I wasn't sure that she believed me. I had no idea how conversant she was with Czechoslovakian literature.

By the time we got down to the town again, it was five o'clock. I asked Beate if she wanted to have dinner with me at the hotel. I praised the food and the view and said they had an excellent wine from Piedmont. She thanked me but excused herself, saying she had something to do.

'Tomorrow we could go to Pogerola,' she suggested.

I nodded. 'Then we can bathe in the waterfall,' I said.

She pinched my arm tenderly and laughed.

We arranged to meet in front of the cathedral at ten-thirty. It would be Easter Sunday.

★

I sat up pondering my meeting with Beate until far into the night. It had been an extraordinary meeting, the sort that only happens once or twice in a lifetime.

She might possibly be the same sort of age as Maria when I'd known her. Maria had been ten years older than me, and now I was the elder. I might be fifteen or twenty years

Beate's senior, but I carried my years well. It was frightening. I was forty-eight, but those final eight years didn't show. 'A bit older,' she'd said. I'd never been embarrassed that Maria was ten years older than me, and she'd never been concerned that I was much younger.

I couldn't believe that Beate was acting as a decoy for a hired assassin – or that she was an assassin herself. But if she had been, she might well have behaved just as she did this afternoon. She'd been in Amalfi exactly as long as me. Perhaps I was easy meat. Tomorrow we'd walk up to the valley and over the mountains to Pogerola. The excursion was her idea, she'd been through the Valley of the Mills to Pogerola before. She hadn't wanted to have dinner with me because there was something she had to do. Perhaps, I thought, she had to make a few phone calls, and presumably there would be men with earphones all over Valle dei Mulini next morning. I could see them in my mind's eye, I could imagine them taking up their positions amongst the ruins of the old paper mills. I could already hear Beate's laughter and I'd long since conjured up a picture of the wad of notes that would change hands. I had a hyperactive imagination.

I glanced up at the portrait of Ibsen. Mightn't the truth just as easily be that Beate and I were two shipwrecked souls clinging together? I thought of Fru Linde and the lawyer Krogstad. They were practically part of the fabric of this room. I was convinced that Beate had something dark in her past as well. Was the idea of a future together so unthinkable? She was living in a bed-sit in the town and was a painter. She didn't know that I was very rich, that was one of the last things I'd tell her.

She was sitting on the cathedral steps at half past ten the next morning. She was wearing her yellow dress again, and I thought that perhaps we even resembled one another in something as mundane as our attitude to clothes. While I was on my travels, I always wore my clothes for as long as possible before putting them out for washing. But maybe the explanation was simply that she particularly liked her yellow dress. I did too. And it was Easter, and for all I knew she might have washed it since yesterday afternoon, it might have been one of the things she'd had to attend to. However, her white sandals had been replaced by a pair of stout trainers. We were going walking.

She rose from the steps and came to meet me. First, we climbed back up all the steps again and stood outside the door listening to the singing from the Easter mass. Beate was solemn and impish at the same time.

We found the alleys that led out of town and, as we ascended the steep hillsides between the lemon groves, she told me she'd never met a man she'd felt so in tune with as me. I returned her almost startling admission and added that, apart from a few short-lived relationships, I hadn't been really fond of anyone since I'd been quite young. I said with a glint in my eye that I'd been waiting for her. Again our conversation was punctuated with irony and hyperbole, but today there was an underlying earnestness to it. I felt sure that Beate really did care for me, and I'd told her I was leaving Amalfi on Wednesday.

I enquired whether it was quite by chance that she'd turned to me for a light the day before. She gave a mischievous smile, but nodded innocently. And had she followed me up to the Valle dei Mulini? She shook her head but said that she'd guessed I was going for a walk and that it wasn't very difficult to work out which direction I'd take as there was only one valley to walk in. So, I said, it was fortuitous that she'd asked if I had a match, but not that she'd walked the same way as me afterwards?

'I suppose not,' she replied enigmatically.

I wanted to get to the bottom of it, and now not simply because I was thinking of Luigi. 'We hadn't even talked to each other,' I pointed out, 'we'd barely exchanged a glance.'

At first she laughed, and then she gave me a completely different version. 'You may be an observant man, but you don't seem to know much about yourself,' she said. 'Well, for a start, you came into the pizzeria with the *Corriere della Sera* under your arm, so you were presumably an Italian, and perhaps even something as rare in these parts as an intellectual. Then you sat down and glanced at me. Your look didn't say much, but it did at least tell me you weren't gay. You ordered pizza and beer, so perhaps you were a tourist after all, but you obviously spoke Italian. You squinted in my direction again, but I think this time you only looked at my feet and took in my white sandals. I attached importance to this detail because not all men look at a woman's feet, but you did. You let your gaze dwell on my feet, you examined my sandals, so you had to be a sensuous person. Then you opened your newspaper at the culture section, and so, perhaps, you were a man interested in culture.

'Once again you looked at me, it was just for an instant, but it was a fixed and level glance. Perhaps you don't remember, but I returned your gaze on that occasion. However briefly, it was the first time you and I looked into each other's eyes, it was our first intimacy, because looking into a person's eyes without averting your own – as one usually does when eyes accidentally meet – can be very intimate. It was a reciprocated look. This time I suspected you of trying to guess my age, but I may be wrong there.

'I'd finished my lasagne and was trying to light my cigarette with a lighter that had run out of gas. You noticed that, but not, I think, that I'd registered your interest. It all took just long enough, perhaps five seconds, so that if you'd had a lighter on you, you'd almost certainly have come across to my table and given me a light, at least if you were the kind of person I took you for. Instead, I was the one who got up and went over to you and asked if you'd got a match. You understood my Italian, but you marked me down as a foreigner because of my accent. You said you didn't smoke, but in a couple of moments you'd picked up a lighter from the neighbouring table and lit my cigarette. You weren't the type just to refer me to the next table, you took responsibility yourself, or rather, you had nothing against lighting my cigarette, you were pleased I'd turned to you. You showed by the way you did it, that it most certainly wasn't the first time you'd lit a woman's cigarette.

'When I thanked you, a shadow fell across your face telling me you were in difficulties of some sort, that you were close to seeking someone to confide in and that that other person might as well be me. I turned and went back to my table, it only took a moment, but I felt your eyes on my back, although that might have been purely my imagination. When you'd paid your bill and got up to go, you gave me an almost sorrowful look and waved, and the way you waved told me that you thought we'd almost certainly never see each other again. I'd been sketching you on my pad because I really liked your face, but you weren't observant enough to notice you were my model. But still I smiled at you with an exaggerated openness. I wanted my look to tell you that our lives are strange; and so you left, but it was as if you took away with you something that you'd glimpsed in my eyes. The way you walked out of the pizzeria told me you were going to the Valle dei Mulini, and of course I could have been wrong, but as it turned out I wasn't. I thought that if I got another chance, you were someone I'd like to get to know better.'

I halted on the narrow footpath and clapped my hands a couple of times. 'Bravo!' I exclaimed. I felt naked and exposed and it felt good, it felt good to be seen and known, it was like coming home. It had been a very long time indeed since I'd had anyone to come home to.

'First you told me you asked me for a match by chance,' I said, 'but now you say you realised I had none.'

She laughed at this small contribution. It was a token that I'd weighed every word she'd uttered. 'Well, it was pure chance that my lighter was empty, but you were no chance person, you were like an open book, a book I'd already begun to read.'

Or she'd been well briefed beforehand, I thought. But I quickly dismissed the idea.

It was for other reasons I said: 'Have you got other lighters?'

She didn't know what I meant. 'Do you always go round with one lighter that works and another that's empty?'

She looked up at me and gave me a little slap. I probably deserved it.

We walked slowly on. The more two people have to say to one another, the more slowly they walk. She went on talking about her watercolours and the exhibition. She told me now that she'd illustrated a couple of children's books plus a de luxe edition of *Grimm's Fairy Tales*. Over the past few years she'd also begun to write.

I was taken aback. I was startled that it was only now she owned up to being a writer, but as she had spoken the last few words with a certain reticence, I decided to refrain from comment just then. Many people feel a bit shy about admitting they're trying to write. Perhaps it was bashfulness that had prevented her from mentioning it the day before.

I told her I'd come to Amalfi from the Bologna Book Fair. I studied her carefully, but she gave no special reaction to my information. I'd have to stop thinking about Luigi. 'So you publish children's books as well?' she asked. I merely nodded. I placed a hand on her head and stroked her hair. She made no comment.

By the time we'd got up to the Via Paradiso half an hour later, we could see that some large, black clouds had begun rolling in across the valley from the encircling mountains. It was sultry. We heard the church bells begin to ring down in Amalfi. A second later the bells of Pontone began to sound as well, and from the ridge on the other side of the valley, those of Pogerola. It was noon on Easter Sunday.

We heard the first growl of thunder, and Beate took my hand. I asked if she wanted to turn back, but she was absolutely set on continuing. She has an appointment with people further up the valley, I thought, and knew that I was imagining things. From the time I'd left Bologna I'd already stage-managed my own death in twenty or thirty different ways. But Beate wasn't part of any conspiracy. I'd high hopes she might be the one to save me from all inventiveness. I'd begun to anticipate that she might even be able to teach me to live like a human being.

We weren't far from the waterfall we'd passed the previous day, when the skies suddenly opened. Beate pointed to the ruins of an old paper mill, and we dashed in to try and find some shelter. We crept as far inside the ruins of the mill as we could. She was laughing like a small child, and her laughter echoed dully. There were a mere three or four square metres of roof above our heads, but the floor we sat on was dry.

Soon we were caught up in the worst thunderstorm I'd ever known, or perhaps I should say the best, because we soon agreed that we liked thunderstorms. They were virile.

The storm lasted more than two hours. The rain tipped

down continuously, but we stayed dry. I said it was back in the Stone Age and we were cavemen. 'There's neither past nor future,' I said, 'everything is here and now.' My voice had assumed a hollow ring. She had nestled into the crook of my arm, and again she asked what my novel was about. I had time to tell her now, she insisted. I let her talk me over. I chose one of the synopses I'd had for sale before Writers' Aid had collapsed. It was a family tragedy. I had the synopsis in my head, and now I fleshed it out. In rough terms the story ran along these lines:

Just after the war, in an old patrician villa in the small Danish town of Silkeborg, there lived a well-to-do family by the name of Kjærgaard. They had just engaged a new servant girl in the house. Her name was Lotte, and that was her only name because she was an orphan of not more than sixteen or seventeen years of age. The girl was said to be extremely beautiful, so it wasn't surprising that the Kjærgaard's only son couldn't keep his eyes off her while she was hard at work for his demanding family. He constantly followed her about the house and, even though he was quite a young boy, he managed to seduce her in the wash-house one day while she was boiling clothes. It only happened once, but Lotte became pregnant.

In the years that followed, a number of different accounts of what had actually happened in the wash-house that fateful afternoon did the rounds. It was whispered that the boy – or Morten, to give him his proper name – had raped the girl as she stood pounding the clothes, but the Kjærgaard family steadfastly maintained that it was Lotte who'd behaved improperly, and that she was the one who'd seduced the boy. Enough witnesses could testify to the way she would giggle and simper and generally behave wantonly in the boy's presence.

The family now made confidential arrangements for the maid to take up a new position with a family in a remote part of the country.

But when, a few months later, Lotte gave birth to a son, they made sure they kept the child as he had the family's noble blood in his veins. Although the Kjærgaard clan was well endowed with worldly wealth, it certainly had no superfluity of heirs, and not a drop of the eminent family's blood was to go to waste. Lotte protested as best she could and wept bitterly when the boy was taken away from her only a few weeks after his birth, but both materially and morally she was considered unfit to look after the child. And, after all, the boy had no father.

Naturally, Morten wanted nothing to do with the baby. He was in any case too young to claim paternity and for their part, his parents were far too old to adopt the child as one of their own children. But Morten had an uncle, who'd long been blighted by a childless marriage, so he and his wife now assumed parental responsibility for the little boy, who was christened Carsten.

Gradually, as Carsten grew up, he would occasionally wonder at the age his mother and father must have been when he was born. His mother must have been nearing fifty, but it never occurred to him that Stine and Jakob, as they were called, weren't his biological parents. On his birthdays he always got a card from 'Cousin Morten', and up to the time of his confirmation, a small Christmas gift sent by post, but of course it never struck him that his eighteen-year-elder cousin was really his true father. It was a well-kept family secret to which he was never privy.

Jakob was captain of a large merchant ship, and when Carsten was small he was sometimes allowed to accompany his father out into the wide world. He became deeply attached to both his parents and, being an only child, they worshipped him above everything else, but when he was in his last year at school, both Stine and Jakob died in a matter of a few months. Suddenly Carsten was alone in the world – and without family, for all four of his grandparents were now dead. By this I mean that as Jakob lay dying, he told his son the old story of the maidservant in the wash-house and cousin Morten, who in reality was his true father.

By this time Carsten had little contact with his cousin. They hadn't set eyes on each other for many years, but when Carsten began to study for his *M.A.* at the University of Århus there came a time when he was completely stuck for money. In his desperation he approached Morten who obviously knew that Carsten was his real son, but who also took it for granted that he was the only person in the world who did, as Stine and Jakob were now dead.

Morten had become a highly respected medical consultant at Århus's hospital. He'd married the lovely Malene, the daughter of a Supreme Court judge in Copenhagen, and they had two nice daughters who both sang in the church choir, and Morten had no intention of initiating his cousin into his spotless bourgeois existence – he knew too much about the boy's chequered family background.

Without letting on what he knew, Carsten asked his cousin for a loan, or preferably an allowance of five or ten thousand kroner, because he knew that his cousin was a wealthy man. But Morten flatly refused Carsten's request; he brushed aside the young student's humble entreaty for a little help in a tight spot. He poured him a glass of malt whisky, made some witticisms about the old days and put five hundred kroner into his hand before packing him off with a few general platitudes about advancement being the reward of study. What proved so fateful was that Carsten – who already had feelings of near hatred for his real father because of his years of dissimulation – now rounded on his cousin, looked him straight in the eye and said: 'Don't you think it's disgraceful to refuse your own son a loan of a few thousand kroner? Perhaps next time I ought to speak to Malene . . .' Morten started, but Carsten had already turned his back, merely remarking as he left: 'We'll say no more about it now!'

After several disrupted years of study, Carsten met Kristine who, from then on, became practically the sole object of his attention. He only rang Morten and Malene a couple of times in the following years, and on both occasions it was Morten who answered the phone. One thing was certain: Carsten would never again ask his cousin for money. Nevertheless, he received cheques from him once or twice, and when he and Kristine were married they got a cheque for five thousand kroner from cousin Morten and Malene, Maren and Mathilde. This was not enough to mollify Carsten's bitterness towards his biological father, and by the time they got married he had decided to adopt Kristine's surname. Her family had accepted him with open arms.

Carsten loved Kristine, and from the moment he met her he never wanted anyone else. But where destiny blunders, no human prudence will avail: Carsten had always had a nasty birthmark on his neck, and when this suddenly began to bleed, Kristine insisted he went to a doctor and got it seen to. The local doctor removed the birthmark and sent it for routine analysis to the hospital at Århus, but unfortunately the result of the tissue biopsy was never sent back to Carsten's doctor. When weeks and months passed without any word from the doctor or the hospital, neither Carsten nor Kristine gave the birthmark another thought. The next spring, however, Carsten fell ill; he was diagnosed with a cancer that was spreading, and this was immediately linked to a tissue biopsy that had been sent to the hospital several months earlier.

Much later, the hospital admitted that the sample from Carsten had been received and analysed and also positively diagnosed as a malignant melanoma, but the mystery about why Carsten's doctor hadn't been informed still remained. The official responsibility lay with the consultant, Morten Kjærgaard, but apparently he hadn't had anything to do with the analysis itself, so it seemed likely that one of the pathology lab technicians had been careless. The local newspaper carried a short piece about 'the consultant who hadn't been told' and who therefore 'was robbed of the chance to save his own cousin'. But it was soon forgotten.

Carsten only lived a few weeks after he became ill. He spent most of the time at home, and Kristine and her parents nursed him as best they could, both physically and spiritually. In addition, a nurse – who was soon visiting daily – provided as much help and support as *they needed. Her name was Lotte. When Lotte learnt just where the unsightly birthmark had been, she looked at Carsten's date of birth again. This was just a few days before he died, but from that moment on she sat continuously by his beside tenderly holding his hand until it was all over. Carsten's last words when he opened his eyes and saw Lotte and Kristine for the very last time, was: 'We'll say no more about it now!'*

I sat cradling Beate in my arms and spent more than an hour over the story of Carsten. She didn't say a word, I could hardly hear her breathing. It was only when I'd finished that she looked up at me and said that the story was wonderful, but also terrible as well. She said it was both wonderful and terrible at the same time. She was a grateful listener. As I'd got a fully fledged synopsis to work from, it wasn't too difficult to fill in the story, especially when I was with Beate amongst the ruins of an old paper mill, constantly being charged by the power and drama of a huge thunderstorm. Again she said that it was sure to be a brilliant book and that she was certain it would come out in Germany too. She said she was looking forward to reading it.

The thunder and lightning continued, and the rain fell just as heavily as before, but the story I'd told gave so much food for thought that I could hardly begin a new one. Besides, it would have been stretching credulity a bit to be working on two novels at once.

We sat talking over certain details and aspects of the plot. I gave Beate the impression that she was offering me valuable advice and, had I really wanted to write that novel, I'd certainly have found the points she raised useful. She nestled closer to me, put one of her hands in mine and kissed my throat a couple of times. It might have been me who began kissing more passionately, but she reciprocated. 'Are we being naughty, now?' she whispered, and then she undressed. In the blue, stormy light she reminded me of a nude by Magritte. We laid down gently on the stone floor.

We had no choice. We were defenceless against the elements. It would have been an expression of moral degeneracy not to have made love in that thunder, in that storm. It would have been like not hearing nature's voice, not bowing to nature's will.

We lay in a close embrace until the thunder died down. The scent of plums and cherries was about her, and no words were needed. Only when it had stopped raining did she half sit up and say: 'Let's take a shower!' It was a rather paradoxical thing to say just as the shower had stopped and all the water had been used up. But she rose and pulled me after her. We ran naked to the path, it wasn't cold. Beate led me in the direction of the waterfall and reminded me of my promise. A few moments later we were standing under the waterfall singing. Beate had begun it. She sang 'Tosca's Prayer', which I thought was a strange choice, so I answered with the much more apposite 'Tower aria'. But she went on with 'Tosca's Prayer': *Perché, perché, Signore?* I appreciated her familiarity with operatic literature. It didn't surprise me, but I appreciated it. I don't know why I suddenly began singing an old nursery rhyme, perhaps it was because I felt so happy. It hadn't entered my mind since I was a boy, but the words went: *Little Petter Spider, he climbed on to my hat. Then down came the rain and Petter fell off splat. Then out came the sun and shone upon my hat. And woke up Petter Spider who climbed on to my hat.*

We ran back to the ruins and got dressed. And by the time we were back on the path, the sun was shining. We felt no shame. The only thing that was a bit embarrassing was that I'd sung the old rhyme about Little Petter Spider. Luckily, she didn't enquire about what I'd been singing, and perhaps she hadn't been listening properly, but I rued my thought-lessness. Once again I was back on the Piazza Maggiore in Bologna.

We crossed the river and began to climb a steep hillside where Beate's trainers really came into their own. An hour later we'd arrived at a viewpoint called Lucibello. From here we looked down on Amalfi and far across the Sorrento Peninsula. Beate stooped and picked a large bunch of birdsfoot-trefoil, which she offered to me. 'There you are,' she said, 'some Easter flowers.' I told her that another name for these yellow pea flowers was babies' slippers, and I showed her why.

We began to descend towards Pogerola. I had the babies' slippers in one hand and Beate in the other. At one point Beate said that we could get married and have children. She didn't mean it, but it was sweet of her to say it all the same. She intended it no more literally than when she'd spoken about bathing together in the waterfall the previous day. I replied by telling her that I'd been thinking about inviting her to go to the Pacific with me. Beate just looked at me and laughed. But now I'd broached the subject.

At Pogerola we went to a bar and ordered a sandwich and a bottle of white wine. We sat outside enjoying the view, we had coffee, limoncello and brandy. I got a glass of water for the babies' slippers.

As we began to walk down the broad stone steps towards Amalfi, she said: 'You write novels, but didn't you also say you work for a publishing company? Isn't that a difficult combination?'

She wasn't chatting now. She wanted to know who I was.

I decided to tell her just enough for her to be able to recognise me as The Spider if she'd ever heard of the phenomenon. I said I helped other authors to write. I mentioned that I sometimes gave them ideas for things to write about, I might even supply them with notes that they could build on. 'I've always had more imagination than I could use myself,' I said, 'it's a cheap commodity.' I said that. I said imagination was a cheap commodity.

Beate's reaction was obvious – she responded with silence and introspection. There could have been several reasons for this. She could finally have identified me as The Spider, or she might indeed be part of the conspiracy. At least it could be assumed she'd read the little article in the *Corriere della Sera* – she'd said herself it was important to read this particular newspaper to keep reasonably abreast of things – and she'd made special reference to its cultural section. But her reaction wasn't necessarily linked to anything she'd heard about a 'spider'. She'd had enough to react to anyway – I'd described a pretty bizarre occupation.

I talked a bit more about fantasy and helping authors. Occasionally she'd shake her head, as if she were becoming more and more pensive. I made a radical decision. I said I wanted her to read something I'd spent the past few days writing at the hotel. I said I could translate it into German for her. I didn't want to keep any secrets from Beate, there had to be an end to all this pretence. I thought again about the two of us travelling and settling down on a different continent. Perhaps we were both running away from something – she'd already moved to southern Italy for the summer. I'd decided to try to live the rest of my life as a decent human being. I'd only got one life, and now I wanted to live out the remainder of that existence.

It was six o'clock. My legs were a bit weary after all the wine and walking, and we decided to sit out on a bluff and watch the sunset. Beate said little, but soon I launched out into a lengthy fairy tale. I didn't often look at her during the course of the story and maybe this was because it took shape as I spoke. I can't remember all the details, but these were the outlines of the story:

Once long ago, in the town of Ulm on the River Donau, there was a large circus. The ringmaster was a handsome man who soon became inordinately fond of the beautiful trapeze artiste, Terry. He proposed to her, and a year later she bore him a daughter, who was christened Panina Manina. The little family lived happily together in a pink caravan, but the idyll was to be short lived, for just a year after her daughter was born, Terry fell from the trapeze and was killed instantly. The ringmaster mourned his wife ever afterwards, but at the same time became more attached to his daughter as she grew up. He was glad, naturally, that Terry had managed to bear him a child before she was suddenly snatched away. He had been bequeathed a living image of his wife for, as the days and the weeks passed, his daughter gradually grew more and more like her mother.

From the age of eighteen months she would occupy one of the best seats at the circus and watch the performance intently. During the intervals she would sometimes get a lick of candy-floss from one of the clowns, and before she was three she could find her way to and from her seat without help or assistance. Soon both audiences and artistes began to regard her as the circus mascot, and it wasn't unknown for people who'd already been to the circus to come back again just to see Panina Manina, because she was a completely new experience every night – you could never predict what she'd get up to. And so the audience always got two performances for the price of one: they watched the evening's show, but they also sat watching Panina Manina.

It wasn't unusual for the little girl to clamber over the wall of the ring and take part in the performance itself. She was allowed to do this because the ringmaster felt so sorry for his poor little daughter, who'd lost her mummy, that he wished her all the happiness she could find. These special contributions were always totally spontaneous. Suddenly the roly-poly little child would get caught up in one of the clowns' routines, or she might run into the ring between acts and do her own little piece, perhaps with a ball she'd borrowed from the sea-lion, a couple of bowling pins she'd wheedled from the jugglers, a hula-hoop, a small trampoline or a spoof water-pistol she'd found in the props store. Panina Manina always got a great round of applause for these ad lib performances and, as time passed, the feeling of excitement before a show had more to do with what the ringmaster's daughter might get up to, than with the long list of acts in the circus programme.

Only the Russian clown, Piotr Ilyich, was unhappy with the state of things. He disliked Panina Manina breaking into his routines, and it annoyed him that she almost always got the loudest applause. He made up his mind to put an end to this nonsense, and one day in the interval he had her abducted. As usual Panina Manina had approached the clown as he stood selling candy-floss outside the big top, but this time he had an accomplice in the shape of a Russian woman who was visiting the town. Her name was Marjuska, and she'd been paid by Piotr Ilyich to take Panina Manina back to Russia with her. And so it came about that the unfortunate girl grew up on a poor farm near a small village deep in the Russian tundra. The woman was never nasty to Panina Manina because she'd always yearned for a daughter, but the girl missed both her daddy and the circus so much that she cried herself to sleep every night for a year. Until one night she forgot why she was crying. But still she went on crying, for Panina Manina was still just as sad, the only difference now was that she didn't know why. She no longer had the faintest memory of the circus she'd come from, forgotten was the smell of sawdust, and forgotten, too, the notion that she had a father in a far distant country.

Panina Manina grew up to be more and more beautiful until at last she was the loveliest woman east of the Urals. This was at the time Stalin ruled Russia, but her foster-mother was a trusted member of the Communist Party and one day Panina Manina moved to Moscow where for a couple of years she earned her living as *a model for some of the Soviet state's greatest artists. Coincidence – and life's coincidences is what this story's all about – coincidence dictated that one summer's day she arrived in Munich, not far from Ulm. Now, her father's circus had come to Munich, and as Panina Manina went about taking in the Bavarian capital, it happened that she caught sight of the big top. She walked towards it, indeed it was almost as if something drew her towards it, but still she couldn't remember that she'd once been a true circus girl herself, for the tent was now in a different town. But deep down inside her there must have been something that recalled the ring with all its clowns and processions, the wild rides and the trained sea-lions. A large crowd had gathered outside the tent as it wasn't long to the start of the evening performance. Panina Manina went to the ticket window and bought the best seat she could get, for she'd travelled far, and in those days it was a great treat for a Russian girl to watch a modern circus in Munich. In the covered way leading to the big top she bought a stick of candy-floss, and though it was a bit odd for an elegant woman to be seen sitting in the front row licking a stick of pink candy-floss, Panina Manina had been determined to try the sweet confection – it wasn't exactly everyday fare where she came from. The performance began: first the great procession with all the animals in the ring, followed by the most daring of trapeze acts, then clowns and jugglers, bareback riders and trained elephants.*

Suddenly, during a short break between two acts something extraordinary happens. All at once, Panina Manina loses control of herself, climbs over the barrier and runs out into the circus ring with candy-floss in one hand and a wide-brimmed woman's hat in the other. She begins to dance and jump about, but she isn't dancing as you'd expect a grown woman to dance. Panina Manina gallops uncontrollably around the ring the way a small child might run about a large floor. At first the audience breaks out into peals of laughter, thinking that this is the start of another funny act, but when the good citizens of Munich – who are renowned for their prudishness – realise that the woman with the hat and candy-floss is just mad or drunk or perhaps even high, they begin to hiss. For a few seconds more Panina Manina is in ecstasy, then she catches sight of an imposing man standing before the large orchestra holding a riding whip. It's the ringmaster. Panina Manina sinks down into the sawdust, she begins to sob and then to weep miserably, because now she's beginning to understand what a fool she's made of herself. In that same instant the ringmaster realises that the hysterical woman is his daughter. He strides across the ring towards her, she looks up at him, and now Panina Manina also remembers that she's the ringmaster's daughter, for blood is thicker than water. The ringmaster decides to cancel the rest of the performance. He looks up at the conductor and tells the orchestra to play the melody 'Smile' from the Chaplin film Modern Times. *And so he sends the audience home. He thinks he's probably finished as a ringmaster because Munich's populace seldom overlooks a* faux pas, *but the ringmaster is happy all the same. He has found his own dear daughter once again, the greatest of all circus tricks, and now he will spend the rest of his life with her.*

Beate hadn't uttered a word while I'd been speaking. She seemed all but paralysed, and when I'd finished and looked in her direction, she appeared dejected. I tried to cheer her up by saying that the story had a happy ending, but she remained glum. Before I'd begun to narrate she'd been holding my hand, but soon after she'd dropped it. I was surprised that a fairy tale could have such an affect on her.

She was taciturn and sat there almost tight-lipped. Eventually she asked me how old I was. I said I was forty-eight. 'Exactly forty-eight?' she asked, and her tone was frigid. I couldn't see why the extra months made much difference, but perhaps she was keen on astrology. I said I was a Leo and had turned forty-eight at the end of July.

We began walking down towards the town. She wore a resigned, almost injured, look. 'Perhaps you'd hoped I was a little younger?' I asked. She just snorted and shook her head. She said she was twenty-nine, and I realised she was exactly the same age as Maria had been in the summer of '71. Time had stood still, I thought, and now Maria had returned. It was Easter Sunday, and Maria had risen from the dead. It was an alluring thought.

Beate's mood had changed totally. She didn't need to be part of any conspiracy to have heard of The Spider, I reasoned. She had one foot in the book industry herself, and down in the valley she'd confided to me that she'd begun to write, and it might well be that what she'd heard of The Spider wasn't particularly flattering. For all I knew she might be the daughter of one of the authors I'd helped. I recollected that at least one of them lived in Munich, a man in his mid-fifties whose family I knew nothing about.

It was a tense and difficult situation, but I felt sure we could get over whatever was troubling her if only I could discover what it was. I'd managed to surmount unpleasant situations before. Beate had told me that her mother had died suddenly only a few months earlier and that she'd been very attached to her. It was hardly surprising that she suffered from mood swings. I'd once lost a mother myself.

We walked past a farm where a couple of dogs snarled, and some fussing geese waddled about a dirty coop. Just before we took the last steps down to the main road, Beate stopped and looked up at me. 'You shouldn't have told me that story!' she exclaimed. Then she burst into tears. I tried to comfort her but she just pushed me away.

'Was it really *that* sad?' I asked.

'You shouldn't have told me that story,' she repeated. 'It was stupid, terribly stupid!'

She looked at me, lowered her gaze, then peered up at me once more. It was as if I was a ghost. She was frightened and I was the one who'd unsettled her.

I was completely at a loss. I enjoyed being with women I couldn't fathom, but this was no fun at all. I must have touched a raw nerve. Perhaps she'd identified with the ringmaster's daughter – after all, I knew nothing about Beate's past. It wasn't often a story had such a powerful effect, but it had been a long day, a day of many strong impressions.

Suddenly she looked up at me again and there was fire in her eyes as she said: 'We must forget we ever met. We can't tell anyone about this, ever!'

I didn't understand this violent attack. I'd had previous experience of sexual escapades being superseded by a kind of contrition – it was something I'd discovered to be a peculiarly feminine characteristic – but this was quite different. Beate wasn't the sort to take being lulled by a thunderstorm to heart. And if she had felt remorse, she'd surely have kept it to herself, or at least not pushed the blame on to me. It wasn't Mary Ann MacKenzie I'd met in Amalfi.

'We must forget everything, don't you see?' she repeated tearfully, then continued: 'We must promise never to meet again!'

When I didn't respond, she said: 'Don't you understand anything? Don't you see that you're a monster?'

Her anxiety was infectious. Perhaps I was an ogre – the thought had struck me. There had been the vague notion that all my synopses and family narratives were perhaps nothing more than my own macabre tango with a terrified soul.

There was something I couldn't recall, something big and painful that I'd forgotten . . .

She'd stopped crying. Beate was brave, she wasn't a person who wept for show. Now only hardness and coldness remained. I didn't recognise her, I had no idea what sort of cross she had to bear, and now her armour was impenetrable.

'I'm scared, I'm scared for us both,' she said.

Perhaps it was a clue. Perhaps she knew about the plans to kill me, she just hadn't realised that I was The Spider, not until now, not until I'd revealed how I helped authors. It hadn't sunk in properly until I'd told the long tale of the ringmaster's daughter, and still she hadn't been quite certain until I'd divulged my age. She had looked into The Spider's eyes and they weren't just one pair of eyes, but many. They'd frightened her. She'd known The Spider was a monster, but she had allowed the monster to seduce her before she'd managed to identify him. She knew about the plans to kill me, and now she was scared for us both.

We passed the police station and walked in silence through the town. From windows and cornices and small balconies fronting the street Amalfi's washing hung out to dry, T-shirts and bras fluttered in the gentle breeze like the semaphore signals from a simple existence. This humdrum life felt like the promised land to me now, but Beate's steps got faster and faster, it was almost impossible to keep up with her, and she didn't stop before we were down on the seafront. I didn't know where she lived, but our ways parted here.

I touched one of her shoulders, and she seemed to freeze.

'I don't understand,' I said.

'No, you don't understand,' she said. 'And I can't *speak* it either.'

She shook off the hand I'd laid on her.

'Are we never to meet again?' I asked.

'Never,' she replied. Then she added: 'Perhaps one of us must die. Don't you *even* understand that?'

I shook my head. She was out of kilter. Again I thought of Mary Ann MacKenzie. I didn't know what I'd set in train.

'Never again, then,' I said.

But she'd reconsidered. 'Perhaps we *must* see each other again,' she said now. 'In which case it should be tomorrow, but that will be the very last time.'

The frigidity with which she spoke this terrified me. 'Fine,' I said. 'Perhaps you'll come and have lunch with me at the hotel?'

She shook her head. She was bitter, so bitter. Then she said: 'We'll just take a walk . . .'

'Yes?'

'We could go over the hills . . . to Ravello.'

Ravello was a name I recognised. It was in the old house high up in Ravello that Wagner had composed *Parsifal*. It was just before his death; *Parsifal* was Wagner's last opus.

I didn't try to draw her out further, it was too painful for her. I had no strength left either. I'd been unable to say a word at my mother's funeral, that was disgraceful. Since then I'd been caught up in a maze, a maze of my own making, my own prison. I had built that labyrinth myself, but now I no longer knew how to find my way out of it.

I said: 'I've lived a miserable, empty life. You're the only person I've really cared for, you're the only person I really like.'

She went into another flood of tears. People had begun to throw glances in our direction.

A thought streaked through my brain, it was a straw to clutch at. 'You said yesterday that you'd tell me about your father,' I said. 'Do you remember?'

She shivered. Then she thought for a few moments, but her only reply was: 'I've said enough.'

For one brief second she leant up against me, resting her head beneath my chin in the way a puppy sometimes lies close into its mother because the world is just too large.

After all the tears and emotions I was again filled with tenderness towards her. I put my arms around her and kissed her brow, but she pulled away in one powerful movement and gave me a sharp slap, and then another. I couldn't tell if she was angry, I couldn't tell if she was smiling. She simply disengaged herself and was gone.

★

I had no dinner, I couldn't bear the thought of sitting in the dining-room, but luckily I had some biscuits and a packet of peanuts in my room. I seated myself at the desk and went on with my life-story. It was a way of collecting my thoughts, of calming down. I wrote of my meeting with Beate in Amalfi and of our trips to Pontone and Pogerola.

I have been sitting here for hours, the time is two a.m. I've stood for a while in front of the window looking down at the sea beating in towards the Torre Saracena. The little man is still wandering about the room. As he walks he waves his bamboo cane and cries 'Swish, swish!' Though I try not to let it, Metre Man's restlessness is naturally taking its toll on me.

It's two-thirty. Again, I've thought through all that's happened during these past few days, and especially what happened with Beate this evening. I feel cold.

It's three a.m. Something terrible is dawning on me. It's as if I've committed a murder, it's like waking up after running down and killing a child while drunk at the wheel. I'm cold, I feel nauseous.

I can't tell if my imagination is playing a trick on me again. I try to put down what I'm thinking, but my hands are trembling. She said her mother just dropped dead on her birthday, and only a few weeks later I met Beate in Amalfi.

It can't be true, my imagination must be playing another trick on me.

My heart is hammering in my chest. I've been out to the bathroom and had some water from the tap, but I still feel nauseated.

What did she mean when she called me a monster? It was because of Writers' Aid, wasn't it? Or was she referring to something else? I don't even dare to follow the thought through. I could never have brought myself to end one of my own synopses with anything so vile. It would have surpassed even my imagination.

Why aren't we supposed to meet again? She couldn't *speak* it, but she hinted that one of us had to die. I thought she was being hysterical. I asked her to talk about her father. It was just to gain time, but she was startled and claimed she'd said enough.

I feel sick, and it's not the thought of Beate, or even the thought of our intimacy up in the Valley of the Mills that has made me feel wretched. I am the object of my own disgust, I feel sick at the mere thought of myself.

I've been out to the bathroom again and drunk more water. I stood there a long while looking at my own reflection. I had to struggle not to retch into the sink. I, too, have high cheekbones. And I've also got something of my mother's eyes.

It's four o'clock. I've started a cold sweat. Life has shrivelled and shrunk, all that's left of it is skin and bone.

I'd pinned every hope for the future on Beate and now it's all gone.

It was when I told the story of the ringmaster's daughter that she really tensed up. She said that I shouldn't have told the story, that it was stupid, terribly stupid. She didn't say that she'd heard the story before, but perhaps that was what she meant. She hinted that I should never have told the tale of the ringmaster's daughter all those years ago. If she hadn't managed to remember the story herself, her mother would certainly have jogged her memory about the funny man who'd helped her into her dress and told her about the little girl who'd got separated from her daddy deep in the Swedish forests.

Poor Maria has passed away now. She died on 19 February on her fifty-eighth birthday. She wasn't ill, but her life just wasn't meant to continue. She was twenty-nine when Beate was born, and now Beate's twenty-nine. It couldn't be mere coincidence.

Maria was only meant to survive until her daughter was precisely the same age as she'd been when she'd so rashly allowed herself to be seduced by The Spider. Then, both she and her daughter would meet their nemesis, a sentence of shame that was as logical as it was inevitable. At the same time, I would suffer humiliation, too. And thus we'd all be reunited in ignominy and disgrace. I knew from previous experience that ogres and demons were only too adept at working in unison.

I may hear more about Wilhelmine Wittmann tomorrow. But even now I realise that it must be Beate who's been hiding behind that strange pseudonym. That was her secret.

There were enough stories to share during the long years Maria and her daughter lived together. Perhaps some of them had been bedtime stories, for I'd told Maria some nice fairy tales, too. So, the stories I'd conjured up for Maria had assumed a life of their own, and now Beate had begun to take them one by one, first *Das Schachgeheimnis* and then *Dreifach Mord post-mortem*. Maria sent no token until her daughter had grown into an adult, literate woman.

She'd been a bit bashful when she told me she wrote, and

I should be the world's number one expert in that sort of difference. I suppose you feel a trifle awkward publishing a story as your own, when the truth is that it's been snatched from the lips of another person.

Triple Murder Post-mortem. I start, I'm scared by own title. In a way all three of us have already felt the swish of death's scythe. But there are two of us left, three including Metre Man.

I'll have to beg to be allowed to raise up the poor circus girl who's collapsed in the ring. She sank into the sawdust and the ringmaster violated her there. After all those years in exile she'd found her way back to her father, but he'd shown so little understanding of the ways of destiny that he'd desecrated her. He had already run away from the great book circus in Bologna. There would be no more performances.

Maybe in a few hours' time I'll hear the story of a mother and a little girl of almost three who lived for a while in Sweden, but who soon left and moved to Germany. Or perhaps they never lived in Sweden, perhaps the ring-master's daughter was born in Germany; Maria's parents were living there at the time, that was another thing I'd forgotten.

The mistake was that I wasn't kept informed. It was Maria's fateful attempt to get far enough away from the monstrous silk mill, to prevent The Spider ever sinking his fangs into her again. I wasn't even allowed to know the girl's name, that was a dreadful mistake. Every father should know the name of his own daughter.

Another mistake was of more recent origin, and it had been mine. I'd completely fallen for Luigi's prattle about a conspiracy of downtrodden writers. As a result I hadn't introduced myself to Beate properly. The thought that I should ever meet 'Poppet' again hadn't even crossed my mind. I'd hardly even considered how old the little girl must be now, let alone visualised her as a grown-up woman.

It is night, but still I occasionally hear the sound of a scooter down on the coast road. I've been standing for a while watching the light from a boat moving far out. Now and then the lantern disappears in the trough between waves and then appears again. There's a crescent moon, but even though it's on the wane, it sheds a broad stripe of silver across the sea.

I have seated myself at the desk once more. I sit staring at a ridiculous coat-stand in the bedroom. It looks like a scarecrow and makes me feel like a small bird.

All I want is to be a human being. I just want to look at the birds and the trees and hear the children laugh. I want to be part of the world, put all fantasy behind me and just be part of it. First I must ask permission to be something as commonplace as a father to my own daughter. Perhaps she'll see no alternative but to break off all contact with me. I wouldn't find that hard to understand. I'm guilty, but isn't there a slight difference between subjective and objective guilt? What I did to 'Poppet' was careless, but it wasn't wilful.

It's turned five. I've no strength left. That doesn't matter, because I've nothing left to defend.

The ice has begun to crack and the cold, dark depths beneath are opening up. There'll be no more pirouettes. From now on I must learn to swim in deep water.

Metre Man is wearing an almost solemn expression and has taken up position in front of the fireplace. It's the first time I've ever seen him rest his cane on his shoulder as if it were a heavy burden. He looks up at me and says: *'And now? Are we going to remember now?'*

But I think it's impossible to have a clear recollection of something that happened when I was just three years old. I look down at the diminutive figure and say: 'I can't say it with words. I've forgotten the language I spoke then. A small boy is calling to me in a language I no longer understand.'

'But you remember something?' the little man asks.

'It's like a film,' I say. 'It's like a few frames of cine-film.'

'We must write the synopsis of that little clip, then,' Metre Man says.

I swallow. But this will be the very last synopsis, I think, as my fingers begin to tap:

Oslo in the mid-1950s, autumn. Three-year-old Petter lives in a modern block of flats with his mother and father. His father has a job in the central tram depot, and his mother works part-time at the City Hall.

Stills of family idyll, ten or twelve seconds from a picnic at Lake Sognsvann, Sunday outing to Ullevålseter etc. Stills of mother and father greeting the new neighbour on the ground floor. He's got a Labrador.

Early morning: father and Petter are in the hall with their coats on. Mother (in her dressing-gown) emerges from the kitchen with packed lunches for both of them. She puts Petter's inside the little blue kiddie's satchel that hangs on his shoulder and does it up. She fondles Petter, kneels down and kisses his cheek. Mother gets up again, gives father a light kiss on the lips and hopes he'll have a good day.

Father and Petter on the bus. Petter asks why he has to go to nursery school. Father says that he has to go to work to make sure all the trams are working properly, and mum must go to the launderette to wash clothes and visit the hairdresser's too. Petter says that he could accompany his mother to the launderette and hairdresser, but father says that Petter has got to go to work as well. Petter's job is to be at the nursery school and play with the other children. Father thinks a bit and then assures his son that children's play is just as important as adults' work.

When they get to the nursery school, they find a notice pinned to the door saying that the nursery school is closed because both the nursery assistants are ill. Father reads the note out loud to Petter. He takes his hand and says that he'll bring him back to Mum. They go into a delicatessen and buy fresh rolls, slices of saveloy sausage, some pickled gherkins and a hundred grams of vegetable mayonnaise. Father says that he hasn't time to eat this lovely lunch himself, but it's for Petter and Mum.

Father and Petter on the bus again. Both are in high spirits, Petter presses his face to the window and looks out at all the people, cars (at least one taxi), bicycles and a steam-roller (i.e. the big, wide world outside the nuclear family).

On the way from the bus stop father begins to whistle the tune 'Smile' from the Chaplin film Modern Times.

They walk up the stairs of the block, Petter is looking forward to getting home to mother. Father unlocks the flat door. Mother comes rushing out of the living-room hugging her dressing-gown. She's horrified and almost stark naked. Pandemonium.

Petter's POV, from three feet above ground level: father and mother scream and yell and say horrible things to each other. Petter screams too, trying to drown out the grown-ups. He flees into the living-room where he finds their new neighbour getting up off the large rug. He's got no clothes on either, they're lying in a heap on a Persian pouffe in front of a teak shelf on which is an old radio set (Radionette), but he covers himself with a musical score (i.e. the anthology Opera Without Words*).*

Scene like something from the silent films, with much shouting and cursing (Petter's POV), but without discernible words. Mother and father have entered the living-room. Father hits mother, causing

*her to fall and bang her head against an old white piano. Blood
begins to trickle from her mouth. The neighbour tries to intervene,
but father rips the phone out of its socket and hurls it in his face.
Neighbour clutches his nose. Everyone is crying and screaming, even
Petter. The only thing that can be heard is bad language, some of it
very bad. Petter tries to outdo the adults by using the rudest words
he knows.*

*Petter starts crying. He rushes out on to the landing and down
to the ground floor. He goes out into the courtyard and rings
all the bells, the whole time screaming: 'POLICE CAR,
FIRE ENGINE, AMBULANCE! POLICE CAR,
FIRE ENGINE, AMBULANCE!'*

*He runs back into the lobby and down the steps to the cellar.
BOMB SHELTER is printed in green, luminous letters above
the cellar door. Petter opens it and creeps behind some bicycles. He
cowers there without making a sound.*

Petter is still crouching behind the bikes. A long time has elapsed.

*Mother comes into the cellar and finds him behind the bicycles.
Both are in floods of tears.*

The boy can't remember any more, and I can't force him. I
can't even be sure if what the boy remembers is true.

Metre Man has dropped his cane on the floor, or perhaps
he has laid down his wayfarer's staff for good, because he
doesn't pick it up again. He just stands there staring up at me
with a wistful, almost dismal air. Then he says: *'We'll say no
more about it now!'*

The next second he's gone, and I know I'll never see him
again.

I'm looking down at a floor covered with tiles. They're
alternately red and olive green. I've begun to count them.

I've picked out a square of four tiles in the middle of the
floor. They lie there glowing so richly on their own that

they seem to outdo the rest of the floor, but they are too tedious to concentrate on for long. I isolate nine tiles, three by three is nine. This too is dull. How could nine ceramic tiles have anything to tell me? I've marked out a square of sixteen tiles, each individual tile is part of a greater whole. They don't know it themselves, but I do. It's irrelevant anyway, because I've already picked out a square of twenty-five tiles. I write B, E, A, T and E on the five topmost tiles. I try to make a magic square out of the five letters. I try it with M, A, R, I and A too, but both are so complicated that I decide to postpone it until I've got more time.

The floor is so big that I have no difficulty in forming a square of thirty-six tiles – I only need to kick a pair of shoes out of the way. These thirty-six tiles belong to the hotel, but their deeper significance is mine. It's unlikely that any hotel guest has noticed this harmonious square before me. It is I who have elevated it to a higher plane, to the realms of thought and contemplation. This deeper perspective is not on the floor but safely stored within my own head. The thirty-six tiles on the floor can draw an imaginary enclosure from my soul. It's generous of me, I think, to keep track of them. I move my eyes across the thirty-six tiles, horizontally, vertically and diagonally. The tiles can't feel me running over them with my eyes. I have begun to concentrate on tile thirteen, it's the first tile in the third row. It has a small chip in the bottom right-hand corner, but it needn't worry about that, I think. There's barely a tile on the floor that doesn't have a blemish of some kind. The tiles are lying on their backs with their faces in the air, and so they can't see one another, covering an entire floor together, but without need of any mutual relationship; at this moment their only relationship is to me, and I examine them all in turn. If I divide tile number thirteen diagonally into two equal halves, I get two right-angled triangles –

isosceles triangles – though of course I haven't touched them. I'm not the sort of person who goes round smashing up fittings, although, if I look at this tile much harder, my stare may crack it. I turn my attention again to the whole square of six times six. There's a lot you can do with six times six ceramic floor tiles – an awful lot, I think. You can write a story about each and every one, that's easy.

I've pushed a chair out of the way and can now concentrate all my attention on forty-nine tiles. I can see all the tiles at once without shifting my glance. I think I must have a special faculty for viewing ceramic tiles. I'm particularly satisfied with this last block, and I'll never forget it: seven times seven tiles is nothing less than the ultimate truth, the answer to the riddle of existence itself. The very kernel of existence is a square of forty-nine green and red tiles in Room 15 of the Hotel Luna Convento, Amalfi. I glance at the coat-stand, but I only have to turn my gaze back to the floor and I see the square again. It hasn't budged even a millimetre, and this is patently because the shape itself is firmly rooted in my mind. It isn't on the floor, but is created by the person who shifts his gaze. If I ever find myself in prison, I'll never get bored while I have this square of forty-nine tiles to think back on. I have glimpsed the world. If I draw an invisible diagonal line from the top right-hand corner, from the top corner of tile number seven, down to the bottom left-hand corner of tile forty-three, it gives me the two right-angled triangles already described. It's just the same as dividing a single tile, because a square is always a square. Each of the triangles has two legs seven tiles long. The sum of the lengths of each cathetus squared is ninety-eight tile lengths, but I'm not capable of working out the square root of ninety-eight. I've been to my cabin bag to fetch my pocket calculator: the square root of ninety-eight is 9.8994949 tile lengths. So now we know, but it seems odd that the diagonal of seven times seven tiles can be such an ugly figure. It might almost be called an ambush, but then chaos has always had a particular talent for destroying the cosmos from within. But now there's something that doesn't add up, something haunting the tiles — and of course, it's the spirit hovering over the tiles that's doing the haunting – but I can't divide forty-nine by two, so how can half the tiles be red and half green? I feel confused, I've begun to doubt my own sanity.

I am saved by an even higher order, a square of sixty-four tiles. I had only to push Ibsen's desk out of the way, though it was heavy and made a noise like thunder, and it is the middle of the night, too. Eight eights are sixty-four, no doubt about it. Now there are thirty-two red and thirty-two green tiles in the square and, without lifting a finger, I've established perfect harmony, I've re-established complete equilibrium between red and green, green and red. I can play chess now, too. Perhaps that was the idea all along. I'm good at playing chess against myself, and I'm good at playing without chessmen and have always been: first, second, third, fourth, fifth, sixth, seventh and eighth rank. I place the white pieces on the first rank: a, b, c, d, e, f, g and h. It's easy, I've got a full view of the whole board, I can see all the squares at once. One at a time I place the pieces on the board. Soon I can see them all quite clearly, they are made of black and white alabaster and are quite large. The biggest ones, the kings and queens, are over thirty centimetres tall.

I'm the white king and I'm in the first row. I'm shown to a red seat – 1E it says on my ticket, a fine seat in the first row of the stalls, I deserve no less. On the great stage before me are ranged all the other pawns and pieces. I find the crowded lists of my own pawns in front of me slightly vexing. They're much too close and smelly, but far off to the left I glimpse the black queen. She's far away on 8D, she's also got a red tile to stand on – a good position as well, I think. I wave at her with my left arm, and she waves discreetly back. She's got a crown on her head, it sparkles in the purest gold.

The chessman have taken their places, and now the game itself begins. I commence with an ordinary king's pawn opening: e2–e4, and she responds equally properly with e7–e5. I move my knight to protect the pawn: b1–c3. Then she makes a surprising move, she moves the queen from d8 to f6, but why? She's combative, she's daring! I move my pawn from d2 to d3 to protect the pawn at e4, and she ripostes by moving her bishop, f8–c5. What plan has the lady got up her sleeve? I move my knight again, c3–d5, and threaten her queen. I do it in order to try to force her to retreat. It's then that it happens, and without my being able to retrieve the situation: the queen comes up and takes a pawn, f6 takes f2. The black queen is at close quarters, holding me in check. She smells of plums and cherries, but I can't touch her, that's the terrible thing. I've committed the worst sin in the chess-player's book, I've not seen beyond the next move, and I've not kept account of previous moves in the game. I've forgotten that the queen has a past, she's of noble lineage, her house is full of silk, and now she has a clandestine bishop on the diagonal from c5 and, in this moment of truth, it is he who prevents the queen from being taken. It's check-mate!

It was a short game, far too short. I was pinned in a corner by the black queen and my game is lost. I'm guilty, not wilfully, but through gross negligence. I'm ashamed. That's the answer, I'm ashamed. And I – who have always pointed out that shame is no longer an element in people's lives – I go off and commit the most outrageous misdeed that any man can be guilty of.

I lay down and have managed to sleep for a couple of hours.

When I opened my eyes it was like waking up to the very first, or the very last, day of my life. I had such a beautiful dream about a little girl who came walking towards me with a big posy of babies' slippers. It was by Lake Sognsvann, or in Sweden by one of the big lakes there. But it was only a dream.

I am at my desk once more, it's nine o'clock. I've done my packing and I'll go down and check out in a couple of minutes. If Beate won't let me leave my cabin bag in her bed-sit, I'll ask if I can deposit it at the police station. I won't leave it at the hotel whatever I do. I'm not the sort who returns to collect things.

I feel something important is missing. Then I realise what it is: when and where was I supposed to meet Beate? We never arranged anything. All the same, I must get out of here, I must escape from my own consciousness.

I'll leave my laptop in the room. I'll lose it here or leave it here, people can wonder which. I've deleted all files that needed deleting, but not the ones that are meant to remain. There are lots of them, an impressive number. There are more than enough synopses and ideas for people to help themselves to, enough for several dozen literary careers, maybe more. I can stick a note to the machine saying that it belongs to all the authors of the world. I could write: here you are, help yourselves, everything is gratis. Then they could do whatever they liked with it, they could just carry on as far as I'm concerned, they could just carry on disporting themselves.

But I change my mind. I write *TO BEATE* on a yellow note and stick it to the machine. For my part, I have no desires other than to be an ordinary person. I only want to look at the birds and trees and to hear children laugh.

Someone is knocking at my door. 'Just a moment,' I call

out, then I hear Beate's voice. She says she'll wait for me down by the convent gardens.

It is the first, or the last, day of my life. I don't know if I dare hope for a miracle. I'll save this and sign off. Everything is ready. Ready for the greatest leap.